Everything You Wanted

There are two sides to everyone...

Heard this book is
KILLER

[signature]

Everything You Wanted

There are two sides to everyone...

Nina Raman

NEW DEGREE PRESS

EVERYTHING YOU WANTED
There are two sides to everyone...

ISBN   978-1-63676-838-0 *Paperback*
        978-1-63730-204-0 *Kindle Ebook*
        978-1-63730-282-8 *Ebook*

Table of Contents:

Note from the Author	11
Prologue	15
Chapter 1	19
Chapter 2	30
Chapter 3	40
Chapter 4	46
Chapter 5	65
Chapter 6	70
Chapter 7	81
Chapter 8	87
Chapter 9	92
Chapter 10	103
Chapter 11	112
Chapter 12	127
Chapter 13	131
Chapter 14	139
Chapter 15	147
Chapter 16	154
Chapter 17	160
Chapter 18	168
Chapter 19	180

Chapter 20   188

Chapter 21   193

Chapter 22   207

Chapter 23   213

Chapter 24   219

Chapter 25   225

Chapter 26   235

Chapter 27   243

Chapter 28   249

Chapter 29   256

Chapter 30   264

Acknowledgments   269

To the future characters I may kill. Run.

Warning:

———

Dear readers,

While I am so very happy that you are reading this book, I have to warn you of some of the events that might take place. Your mental health is important, and I would never wish to inflict any distress upon you, my trusted readers. I wrote this book because I wanted to be honest and open about the struggles of growing up, my family life, and my personal demons. To ignore these struggles would be an injustice to the young adult demographic, and for that I chose to write a story with authentic experiences that may involve violence, alcohol and substance abuse, eating disorders, self-harm, and anxiety.

If these scenes overwhelm you in any way, please take a break, get a snack, go for a walk, and take care of yourself. The book will be waiting for you whenever you're ready to continue reading.

The events of this book are purely fictitious, but I know many people still face these struggles every day. While the characters are a product of my imagination, I know that to many of you they will be real. I hope their inner conflicts help you learn and grow and, most importantly, teach you to take care of yourself.

Best,

Nina Raman

Note from the Author

I went to a really big high school. There were over a thousand kids per grade, and it seemed like I met every type of student in that school. There were the stoners, the jocks, the brains, the born-for-Broadway kids. And then there were kids like me: the average do-gooder.

I always found myself wondering, What would happen if some of these kids decided to do the opposite of what was normal for them? What if the smart kids took a walk on the wild side? Would it be fun and enlightening, or would it make their whole world fall apart?

When you ask people about their high school, it seems like other schools are worlds away from your own personal experience. Everyone acts differently, but my school had a perfect mix of all things that made high school both infuriating and exciting. I was always a good kid who did her homework, ran some extracurriculars, and overall did the right thing. But I wanted to know—what happens when you do the wrong thing?

It is only human nature to wonder "what if?" What if I don't do my homework? What if I go to a party? What if I do something I know I shouldn't? How do people live with these decisions, and how do they impact them from such a young age?

In high school, you're just barely an adult. You can drive, but you can't vote yet. You can get drunk, but not legally. You are always caught in this web of ready, but not yet. Being a teenager makes you want everything and more, so I wanted my main character, Wren, and her best friend, Rohit, to explore what happens if you get what you want and it turns out to be just the opposite.

What are the consequences of a "good kid" doing something bad?

What's surprising is how often scandals happen. We all know how everyone looks at these people after something preposterous happens, but how does it shake the community as a whole? What if it were worse than a simple scandal? What if instead, someone was murdered, and the prime suspect went to school with you? How do people behave when they are dealing with this sort of news?

Everyone seems to believe that murders are typically committed by adults, but what's scary is that anyone can commit them. Imagine if your friend, peer, or enemy was capable of a thing as terrible as murder. Teenagers experience so much adolescent angst and have difficulty exploring who they actually are. Perhaps the version of themselves they are looking for is someone they're better off not knowing.

We meet many people over the course of our lives, but how well do we really know them? Ted Bundy had a girlfriend during the time he raped and killed women. Jeffrey

Dahmer developed his dark obsession while attending high school. Just because we see people every day doesn't mean we actually know them. Who knows what they've really gone through? Most times, those who commit such heinous crimes suffer hardships in their lives. How come we never learn of their challenges until after the crimes are committed? Until after the damage is done? We really don't know people all that well.

The closest we get is when we read their stories in books. We get to see the characters' deepest desires and opinions they wouldn't dare share out loud. I have always loved reading young adult novels, but I have a major problem with them. Most center around teenage love and little snags in relationships. While these fuel our love lust inside, I wanted to do more exploration. What happens to a main character when absolutely everything is at stake?

There is much more to people than what meets the eye. Like the main character, Wren Clements, you might have many layers underneath, and that's okay. Self-discovery is always happening; it isn't just through a few years of your life. Whether you are high school, young adult readers, or middle-aged murder mystery enthusiasts, exploring who you truly are never stops.

I hope you find this story compelling in the sense of learning that people you know can still surprise you, even if you consider them a close friend. Life will take you through many journeys of self-discovery, and this book is just a highlight of an extremely vulnerable part.

Maybe you can relate, or maybe you haven't reached this scary vulnerable part just yet. Whatever it is you end up going through, just know this is all a part of self-discovery. It can be ugly and triggering, but it is situations like these that truly build us to be the people we are.

Keep growing.

Prologue

———

"Why are you here?"

"I didn't know where else to go," she found herself saying, just merely above a whisper. She longed for an escape.

"Did anyone see you?"

"No. No one ever does. I'm careful," she reminded, her fingertips grazing the door frame, slowly inching her way across the threshold.

"Good. Close the door."

Springs shifted under her as she took a seat on the couch. Fresh laundry filled the air, although the room was dull and musty and still layered with dust since her last visit. She felt the paisley stitched fabric under her and groaned at the stain in the corner.

"You should clean this place up a bit."

"Whatever. It doesn't really matter."

"Yeah, but we've been meeting here for some time now. It's gross."

"Why did you call me?"

Her throat closed in a single breath. Every inch of her body was on edge from the news she got earlier that evening.

"Can I have some water?" she croaked.

A minute had flown by in a blink. She resented the way that time seemed to be fleeting with every breath she took. Her hands melted as condensation dripped onto her already clammy fingers. A skeletal shiver ran through every bone. She could almost hear the silence in the air, only cars passing by far off in the distance.

"It was all for nothing," she whispered.

"What?"

"They said 'no.' This whole thing was a waste." A bitter taste filled her mouth. "I should go."

"Can we talk about this?"

"What's there to talk about?" She found her voice raising in a heated fury. "This was a waste of my time!" Something flickered between them. Somehow the air had shifted, and everything was different. A moment of fear and regret washed over her. Her head began to shake as her legs locked in place. "I'm sorry."

"A waste of time? I tried to help you! I put my ass on the line, and for what? For some bitch to tell me I'm a waste of time?"

The space between them closed. They could feel the warm breath of each other.

"I didn't mean it. It just... slipped out." She found herself searching for any reason to take it back.

"You used me. Didn't you?"

She took a step backward, but somehow the distance between them grew smaller. A tight hand wrapped around her wrist and squeezed.

"You're hurting me!" she gasped, trying to unshackle herself from the clasp.

"*Didn't you?*"

"Yes!" she shrieked. "I used you." The hold softened. "I needed your help."

"And you got it. But now what? I'm not enough?"

"I didn't get what I wanted... I should go." She made a dart to the door, but her accuser collided with her and pinned her hard against the door, faster than she could blink.

"Let me go! Please!"

"We're not done talking about this!"

She raised her elbow and drove it into her offender. Although the space between them expanded, the relief only lasted for a second.

She felt a push back. But *harder.*

She was propelled into something stiff and angular that made her head fill with heat and her eyes fill with dark splotches. Her fingertips grazed her scalp. Wet, warm liquid seeped onto her skin. Her fingers shook and carefully retracted from her head. There it was. Red, black, and hot running down her.

The room swayed around her. She felt the buckle in her knees loosen as she collapsed onto the floor.

"H-hel... help... me. P-pl... please."

The air filled with fear and loss and regret and shame. But besides all of that, her mind went to a different place.

She was riding a bike for the first time without the training wheels, the pink and purple streamers floating in the wind as she pedaled into the sunset, laughing. Then she was seven, happy on the school bus. She could hardly hide the skip in her step on her way through those doors. Then she was fourteen and sitting at lunch with new friends who were laughing, smiling, and living.

And then she saw those unforgiving eyes before her. It became much harder to swallow. The weight of a truck pressed on her lungs, and her heart felt like it was going to beat right out of her chest.

"P... please."

"I'm sorry."

And in that moment, she realized that she shouldn't have done it. There was no getting back what she had lost, and there were no real winners in the end.

Chapter 1

———

Wren was painting her nails an eggshell blue when the mailman lifted the mail slot cover and slid a landslide of envelopes through the door. She jumped up, so eager to retrieve the scattered items that she had forgotten to roll up her sweatpants to prevent marks on her freshly pedicured toenails. *At least now my nail polish matches the paint job on the door,* she thought. The black paint was chipping off, revealing a hideous carnival red. The Clements family would never be caught dead with a door that color. The Clements were all about looking polished and, most of all, looking better than everybody else.

She added repainting the door to her list of things to do. Some would think this is absurd, but she was nothing if not a perfectionist. The slot fell back with a clatter as she reached down to the pile of white envelopes to dig out the crimson one with a gold stamp in the corner. Her eyes glistened, eyeing the shimmering gold, longing to dig through the envelope's contents. Her school had been one of the only ones in the area to still send out physical report cards. They were old fashioned like that. It was a public school with a private school guise, one of the things Wren loved so much about it.

So there she stood, her potential future hand. It was her last report card. In a little over a month, she would graduate, wishing her class the best of luck as their salutatorian, and cheering on her best friend Rohit Kumar as the valedictorian.

She tore open the letter suddenly, smudging the nail polish she had spent an hour doing ever so perfectly. Her eyes were hungry for confirmation of her hard work, although she always knew they would be satisfied. All A+'s, except for AP Economics, which had been the toughest subject to take in all of Richmond High. She got an A-. Oh, how easy it was to be disappointed by the tiniest of snags.

The slightly less than perfect grade stared at her, prodding her hard in the shoulder with the force of a sharp knife, but she tried her best to shrug it off. Everybody is susceptible to imperfections. Everybody makes mistakes. Everybody has a weakness. Certainly nothing worth killing herself over. She tried to remind herself of this whenever something like this happened.

She felt a twist in her personality. The disappointment had crawled in during a breath and settled, kicking in her gut. She felt her mind try to change the subject and distract her with something of less significance, but she resented this feeling: the child inside of her, not wanting to care, wanting to move onto the next thing. She got caught up in any sort of thought that wasn't her main focus.

It was acting up a bit more today. The only way to get it out was by taking her pill and coming clean to her parents.

She headed straight to the kitchen and grazed her fingertips through the medicine cabinet to find her prescription of Adderall. One pill a day was the rule, and she always obeyed it. She had only forgotten to take it once, and she had been on edge the entire day, her thoughts popping in and out of her head sporadically.

The Clements were good at focusing on a lot yet never getting distracted. That's why she had to make sure she could tame her ADHD brain. By now she could usually swallow the pill dry, as she had been taking this medication since she was ten, but her throat was unnaturally dry after seeing her report card. She filled a glass of water and took a couple sips before chasing down the yellow pill that took away what made her different. Just as the pill settled, the garage door opened. Her mother and father practically fell through the door with groceries piled up on their arms. Her mother placed the gallons of milk and juice on the marble countertop before noticing her daughter standing with a half empty glass of water.

"Wren, help us unload the groceries," her mother commanded with a hawk stare.

Her parents were lawyers and barely had time to go to the grocery store, so when they did, they bought enough food to feed an army. When they finished unloading the rest of the groceries, her mother switched the coffee maker on to recharge her and her husband. Wren's parents worked both days and nights, but they were more fatigued by shopping at a grocery store than with their demanding jobs.

"Guess what came in the mail today?" Wren spoke, a little afraid but also relieved that high school was coming to a close. Everything that she had worked for, everything she wanted, was ending very soon.

"The books I ordered?" her father inquired, suddenly perking up in his seat.

"No. Uhh…" Wren reached behind her back and pulled the envelope out from under its hiding spot in the back of her sports bra. "The last report card of my high school career," she announced, nerves flailing off of her.

Her parents froze. It was typical of them to act as if someone had just died whenever they heard that news.

"How are your grades?" Her mother glared.

"The same as usual." Wren took a deep breath and exhaled. "But I got an A-minus in AP Econ," she said, her voice growing more faint.

"How come? Did we not get you a beautiful desk in which you can study? Did we not get you a car that you can drive to a library, study group, or to get extra help?"

"No, you guys have done a lot for me. I don't know. To be perfectly honest, I don't think Mr. Alcott likes me very—"

"Wren, you have no one to blame except yourself. God, take some ownership. Do you think Stella Lu or Rohit are blaming others? You're better than this."

Her mother stewed in her coffee, bitter that her daughter had failed her again. She knew that comparing her daughter to her peers was just enough of a kick in the ass.

Her father placed a hand on Wren's knee. His smile was soft and gentle. "Your mother just wants the best for you, sweetie. Even though she may come off a little strong—..."

"Excuse me?"

"Strong-willed, sweetheart. Wren, honey, we know you try hard. But being next best sometimes isn't enough. We just want you to succeed in whatever you do."

"I just want you guys to be proud of me," Wren confessed.

"Then try harder." Wren's mother scoffed.

"We *are* proud of you, Wren." Her father smiled.

The feeling that snuck into her gut had dissolved into nothingness. Just like that, everything was okay. Her dad had that effect on people. The doorbell rang, and her mother went to answer it, leading a beaming Rohit inside with a matching crimson envelope.

"Did you see what came in the mail?" he spoke a little too loud, his voice jumping with excitement.

Wren waved hers in the air and replied, "Yeah, all A-plusses except AP Econ. You?" She asked the question only as a nicety, and Rohit knew that. She already knew the answer. It was the reason why he was valedictorian and she wasn't.

"Don't make me say it. You know I don't like to gloat," he said, grabbing a seat at the table and taking a sip from her water.

"Oh please, you love to gloat. You've been doing it every year since kindergarten. You know I know you better than anyone." She bumped his shoulders with hers as she took the seat next to him. "Go ahead. It's the last time you can do it before we're off to different colleges." He looked at her a little hesitant, and she punched him hard in the shoulder. "C'mon! Be a man. Let me have it!"

"That phrase 'be a man' is completely un-feminist of you. Why not be like a woman?" He retorted with a smile.

Wren rolled her chocolate eyes and snapped back. "Ro, you don't need to tell *me* how to be a feminist."

"Alright. Well, I got all A-plusses. There, I'm tired of gloating." He sighed, and took another sip of her water.

"Tired of gloating? Rohit Ajay Kumar, what the hell happened to you?"

"Well, when I'm at Brown next year, I don't know if my new friends will be as willing to listen to my accomplishments as you are."

"So, I'm the ultimate best friend?"

"Alright, just go grab your stuff you weirdo." Rohit laughed, dodging the question.

Wren went upstairs and grabbed a pink windbreaker from her room with an Eagles hat and tossed it on top of her two Dutch braids. She shouted to her parents that she was going out with Rohit and they hollered back an "okay" as she grabbed her keys and phone and opened the garage door.

She checked the tire pressure of her bike, and when it was perfect she kicked back the bike stand with her foot and wheeled herself out onto the driveway to meet Rohit. They always did this whenever they could. On beautiful days like this, they would bike around town and settle down at the park to do whatever they wanted. Always together, always on bikes.

They set out with the cool spring breeze on their winter speckled cheeks. It had been especially cold that year, and the weather was only now just allowing the slightest bit of warmth to slip through. Outside was a song of chirping of the birds and wind whistling through tree branches, clothed in lush green. Laughter joined in on the song, and the pair biked the same way they had since they were kids, constantly racing to pass the other.

The park was their favorite place to go. Rohit always brought the blanket for them to lay on and look at the sky while Wren bought the ice creams, and when they were old enough, coffee. Their friendship was simple: they sat, they sipped, and they talked their troubles away.

"Remember your first kiss?" Rohit teased, tickling her stomach.

"I remember you *daring* me to kiss Nick Underwood." Wren shoved Rohit's shoulder a little further back than she intended. She was always a little rough with him, and he simply let it happen. Whatever made her happy.

"Yeah, but that wasn't the funny part. It's what you did to actually complete the dare."

"Um, hello? It was the third grade. I wasn't going to kiss twenty bucks away."

"Yeah, I know. You actually kissed him!"

"I remember what I did. I was there, wasn't I?"

"I know. I just like you telling the story." Rohit laughed.

"Well, come here then." Wren tugged on Rohit's shoulders as she pulled his head down to her lap and began stroking his hair like a little baby as she recalled her past embarrassment. Chills flew up his spine. He wished them away before she could notice.

She spoke like a pompous storyteller, adding the flourish of vocabulary here and there.

"I remember sneak attacking him after soccer practice. I tackled him to the ground and pinned him down. His face was flabbergasted by the fact that a girl half his size could be that forceful. He shook, thinking he had the power to shove me off of him, but I was ever so persistent. He moved his face back and forth trying to dodge me, but one punch to his left cheekbone and he stopped. *Boom.* I planted one on him. He resisted, but then he got way too into it. That kid was born a dick, and still is one" She rolled her eyes and continued. "One more punch and he drew back and let me go. Now tell me, do you know anyone else who has completed a dare better than I?"

"Third grade and you had bigger balls than anyone else. Even now." Rohit smirked, taking an extra long look at his best friend.

"Shall I remind you of *your* first kiss?"

He felt a flood of warmth inside, but masked it with a groan.

"Ahh, yes," Wren proceeded. "That was me. Sixth grade, wasn't it?"

He didn't have to think hard about the day when he kissed Wren. The memory was forever etched in his

There are two sides to everyone...

mind. "No fair. I hadn't kissed anyone yet and you were the only girl I was really close with. I just went for it."

"And how did that work out for you?"

"I got punched in the face—"

"-You deserved it!" Wren erupted with laughter that filled the whole park.

"Well, I bought you ice cream the next day to make up for it!"

"You two make a cute couple," a young mom on her walk said.

"We're not—" Rohit started.

"-Thank you!" Wren pulled Rohit's face toward her and kissed his cheek.

The mom smiled and pushed her baby in his stroller back down the sidewalk.

"Why do you like playing these games?" Rohit asked Wren, smudging her cherry Chapstick across his cheek.

"Because it's entertaining. And soon we'll be adults and we'll have to accept the fate of reality. We should have some fun while it lasts."

"Oh, you're so deep." Rohit mocked Wren, tapping his index finger on her nose.

She scoffed, and then time froze for a split second that felt like ten minutes. It was like everything around her had spurred into slow motion, and she was able to live in her thoughts and her own mind for an infinite amount of time. She rose to an epiphany.

"Ro?" He tried to meet her gaze, but she was staring off into the park, still deep in thought. "We're good kids."

"Yeah?"

"Doesn't that bother you?"

"Why should it?"

She rolled her eyes, and he gave her a look. She got annoyed when people couldn't jump to her thoughts at the same exact moment she thought of them. This is why she didn't have many friends. The thought of that sent a shiver down her spine. She pushed Rohit hard in the head.

"Ow!" he complained, even though Wren had intentionally *not* hurt him.

"Do your parents ever tell you stories about their crazy days from high school, where they would break rules, sneak out, and do things they would never do now in their boring adult lives?"

"My parents grew up in India. You got whacked in the head with a slipper for those sort of things."

"That's not the point." Rohit was always making remarks about his traditional, Indian family.

"So what *is* your point?"

"My parents never had those experiences either! We grew up as adults, we aren't growing *into* adults. Do you see where I'm going with this?"

Rohit shook his head.

"Sheesh, Ro. If it takes you this long to figure things out, maybe I should be valedictorian."

He squinted his eyes at her and then flashed a mocking grin. "Okay. I do see what you're saying, but it's too late. We're all grown up now. The only thing we maintain about our childhoods is riding our bikes and coming here. What's so wrong with that?"

Wren's heart broke just a crack. Sometimes, she forgot that she even had a heart. She often thought that her brain and body operated on its own, like a robot with blood running through her veins just as a disguise. "What's wrong with that, Ro, is that they killed us before we had the chance to really live."

"Killed us?"

"Our childhood! We never got to make mistakes and have fun."

"We do have fun......"

"Oh, Thursday night Scrabble is fun? C'mon. I mean really experience what it's like to be a teenager."

"Like drugs, sneaking out, doing other illegal things that could get us in trouble?" Rohit fretted.

"No one's gonna get in trouble. I promise. You worry too much," Wren cooed.

"We can't go behind our parents' backs. Especially my—"

"Yes, yes, I know all about your Indian parents and their dignity. I've heard it before."

"You know, sometimes you interrupt me too much."

"I just know you too well." Wren winked.

Chapter 2

"What you're suggesting is psycho."

"What I'm suggesting is genius," Wren challenged.

"Why do you always assume your ideas are amazing?"

"Because they always are. I even have really good bad ideas."

"I'm not going to lie to my parents." The words tasted sour in his mouth. He hated to disappoint her.

Wren let out an exasperated sigh. "Ro, if you're not even willing to do that, this plan is never going to work."

"We don't even have a plan."

"But we will." Wren winked, determined as ever.

"I don't understand why we need to do this at all."

"Do you want to end up like Stella Lu? Already a freaking robot," Wren pointed out.

"So she works really hard. She just does what she wants. Is that so wrong?"

"She does what she's told. And that's why she's so boring and is already a lost cause."

"Don't make this about your dumb rivalry. High school is almost over. Can't you guys just get along?" Rohit yawned, tired of hearing the same story over and over again.

"No, we can't. I don't want anything to do with her, nor do I want to be anything like her. So c'mon, Ro. We can really have some fun here!"

Wren had spent the entire evening trying to convince Rohit that their entire childhood had been stolen without them even noticing. She desperately wanted it back. Even if it was just for one, reckless night. So much of Wren's life had been planned out for her, and for once she wanted to control something in it. She wanted to feel like a real person. Being anyone else seemed better than getting accepted to an Ivy League school, and it was just because anyone else could afford to make mistakes.

Rohit hadn't given her a chance to come up with a plan. He was too concerned about not being perfect. That's all that mattered with his parents, but Wren cared about him and knew that being perfect wasn't the same as being happy. Rohit was really only himself when he was with Wren. At home he was Rohit, but with her he was Ro. He liked being Ro. That's why he listened to Wren. She didn't give him orders; she encouraged him to break out of his parent-made mold. Of course, when she wasn't around he would mold himself back, but for the time being he could let loose.

"Look. I'm not going to force you into anything." She sighed, still with a flicker of hope in her body that her best friend would come to his senses.

"You're not forcing me." Rohit noticed Wren tugging on her braids and shifting her weight between each leg.

"Hey," he grabbed her hand, "did you take your medicine today?"

Her hand shivered at his touch. It slid out from under his. She hated when he talked about her condition.

"I'm sorry..."

"Yes, *Mom,* I took it right before you came over."

She relaxed her legs again and resorted to drumming her fingers on the grass. She saw Rohit's eyes follow the sound of her fingers tapping away. He knew that sometimes she had days where the medicine didn't work entirely well.

"Quit looking at me like that," Wren snapped, retracting her fingers.

"Sorry." Silence had passed for a while. Wren took out her phone and had gone onto the *Washington Post* when Rohit pushed the phone out of her hand and onto the grass, eyeing her disappointment like a dare. "So how the hell are we going to do this?"

A grin wide as an ocean spread across her slim visage. She knew he would cave. Most men do with her. Among many other things, she was quite talented at sweet talking them. Women, on the other hand, were a whole other species that Wren couldn't even try to get anything out of. Maybe her parents were to blame. Her father was always so sweet and understanding, and her mother... consistently disappointed. It was no wonder why she favored men.

"We can't do this alone. If my parents find out, they're going to threaten to send me to a school in India." Rohit whined, already regretting his approval. His parents were always looming that threat over his head, as if they were ready to ship him off to some rural village if he didn't get 100 percent on his calculus exam.

"Ro, just chill. How many times do I have to assure you that no one is gonna die? You do this every time."

"Do what every time?"

"You know..." Wren raised her eyebrows. "You act like the world is gonna end if you do something different. And I always have to pull you back from your thoughts and tell you that you'll be perfectly fine!" Wren insisted, rolling her eyes.

Rohit rolled his eyes back at her. "Why do you have to make me sound like such a wimp sometimes?"

"I don't make you sound like anything. I'm simply recalling details from the past." Wren batted her lashes, mocking him. "So you want to assemble a team to join us?"

"Well, do you really think we would know where to go, what to do, or who to talk to? We'd probably end up back here doing what we always do."

He had a fair point. Of all the knowledge they had, sneaking out and being rebellious was like a foreign language to them.

"Okay, so who do you think would come with us? Who can give us the full experience?"

And with that, Wren scooped up her phone from the table, flipping through Instagram pages and private Snapchat stories. An hour ticked by quickly, and their list was finalized. They would recruit:

Tyler Harrison—genius stoner boy who sat behind Rohit in AP Calculus;

Sammy Rodriguez—one of Richmond High's most approachable party girls;

Derek Sanders—street painter and spontaneous artist;

Asa Mitchell—Wren's secret crush (the two had been flirty but friendly with each other for years);

Valerie Scott—had a reputation for coming up with the most iconic dares; and

Mia Young—dated a guy who runs a liquor shop.

"How do we approach them? And why would they want to hang out with us?" Rohit questioned.

"They're invited to see some goody-two-shoes kids screw up. You honestly think they would miss that for something else?" Wren suggested.

"Okay. But how do we do this without our parents finding out?" Rohit asked, chewing on his bottom lip.

Wren tugged on her braids again and undid them only to rebraid them. Rohit used to tease her and call her Violet Baudelaire for it, since she did this sort of thing when she had to think. Finally, her eyes brightened with the sudden realization of an obvious answer. Sometimes the easiest solutions were the hardest to find.

"What? What'd you think of?" Rohit asked, eager to see what his best friend saw.

"We don't."

"Huh?"

"We don't hide it from our parents." By the look from Rohit's mortified face, Wren continued to explain her plan. "If we go behind their backs, they'll be angry. Right?" She waited for a nod from Rohit. "So, if we tell them that we are going to sneak out and we'll be responsible, they can't say we lied."

"Wren... this is your dumbest idea ever. My parents aren't going to let me go."

"Yes they will!"

"Easy for you to say, you've got white parents!"

"Ro, would your parents be more mad if you lied, or if you told the truth?"

He rolled his eyes.

"Would they trust you if you were out by yourself, or if you were out with me?"

He sat back down and fiddled with his coffee cup.

"Would your parents let you go if my parents let me go?"

Rohit went quiet for a moment, deep in thought even though he didn't need to think that hard. His parents and her parents were as close as Rohit was with Wren. They always asked each other for advice, and Wren's parents had always been the stepping stone of acceptance into leniency. Wren's parents were the ones who convinced Rohit's parents that it was okay to date in high school, something his very strict parents only thought of in their worst nightmares. They convinced his parents to let him do everything she does. What Wren never let Rohit know was how hard it was to convince her parents to do this in the first place.

Rohit released a heavy sigh and took a sip of his coffee. It had gone cold and bitter, his lips whimpered in response. "Fine. But you need to get them to agree first." And then he downed the quarter of coffee he had left and didn't give it a chance to glaze over his taste buds.

"Deal."

The sun seemed to go down much slower than on their usual bike rides home. A million thoughts buzzed through Wren's mind, thinking of some way to convince her parents that sneaking out was a good idea. She wished it were as simple as how she explained it to Rohit. These things were never easy, but if Wren adored anything, it was a challenge. She lived for people telling her she couldn't do something. She liked the look on their faces when she proved them wrong. She always made her own decisions, and to her parents' delight, they were always good decisions. Until now. But it would be good, healthy even, because breaking the rules was a part of growing up. And if you've been good for so long, it is only a matter of time before you long for something dark.

After saying goodbye to Rohit, she raced up to her room to think up something that would convince both hers and Rohit's parents that they deserved a night out. She closed the door in a hurry, throwing her jacket on a hook and kicking off her Converse. She blew past her beautiful, untouched glass desk and grabbed her laptop to sprawl across the sunny spot on the floor. Wren's mother had gotten her that desk in hopes to inspire perfection, but Wren could never sit still in one place. School already tested her patience too much. She switched from the stiff floor to the chair swinging from the ceiling and tossed a blanket her grandmother made over her knees. She kept this blanket hidden in a drawer, far from her mother's eyes.

"I'm going to donate that," her mother had said firmly one day while Wren was ten. "It's hideous. You need something more grown up," she stated, eyeing the colors and disproportionate measurements.

"No, Mom, please! This is my favorite blanket," Wren cried.

"It's ghastly. Look at it, it doesn't match with anything in this room!" her mother complained.

Lucky for Wren, her father sympathized with her, as he too had an attachment to his mother's hideous blanket.

That blanket stayed in her room ever since. The most unlikely colors were made to come together, like every loose thread or hole gave it character. She liked having something that wasn't as polished as everything else. Her room was so neat, she thought that if she let her mom decorate all of it, it might end up looking like a mental hospital. The walls and furniture were blindingly white, clean from everything abnormal. Wren was careful to place only a few pieces around her room that her mother wouldn't mind. Green plants hung from her window, and white fairy lights twinkled around the perimeter of her room, rushing past her neatly scattered belongings. Class projects and awards hid in the nooks and crannies of her walls as pictures filled the spaces on her nightstand, coffee table, and dresser. Sometimes Wren liked to let her imagination get the better of her. The pictures would come to life and talk as if they were in *Harry Potter.*

She looked at the picture frame on her nightstand.

Her grandmother asked her, "Why can't you act like an ordinary girl? Back in my day, I used to do the craziest things…"

Wren's mother's picture interrupted her. "Oh please, Beatrice. Don't poison her mind. Control your mother, Michael."

Wren's father's image started to talk next. "I mean, is there anything wrong with it?"

"Psst… Over here!" A polaroid of Rohit was speaking. "Don't get me into trouble. Think about our parents! We can't lie!"

"Wren," her mother was blabbing again, "don't you dare lie to us!"

Voices fell over each other into a muddled noise. Wren yelled, as if they could physically be silenced. If she really wanted to do this, she was going to do it right.

She didn't want to lie to her parents, and after all, Rohit didn't have the balls to lie to his.

The truth.

She had focused on the truth before, but now it seemed too difficult of a concept to reach. She set the computer down and replaced its spot with a scrap book. She flipped through, frowning at the sight of every page marked with several awards. They stared at her and mocked her failure to make her plan possible. A bland taste filled her mouth with the dry feeling of emptiness. *So this is what failure feels like*, she thought to herself. Her head shook in disdain. She couldn't accept that she failed so quickly.

Her parents had her frame everything ever since she won her perfect attendance award in kindergarten. Wren's fingertips traced signatures of former principals, stamps of recognition, and different sized awards before flipping to one page heavier than any others. It was an essay she wrote freshman year. She won a contest with that essay. She had written about energy conservation, an overdone subject, but turned it inside out, revealing points that needed to be acknowledged with matching solutions. There was a comment on the essay. It read "Powerful and persuasive" in deep blue cursive lettering. The comment brought a rush of warmth to her face, stretching her lips into a smile. She flipped through it, recalling just how she turned a topic as overemphasized as energy conservation and made it her own. Her ideas could do that, her words could make anything sound... important.

That's when she realized that telling her parents the truth wasn't the obstacle—it was all in the presentation. It was the same with essays. Everyone has the same points, but it's the way each student lays them out that separates the great and the weak. She had forgotten how professional she could be, how she had always made her parents listen to her input in conversations. The idea had come so clear to her now, the same way her medicine had made her head focus instead of its usual jumping nature.

She reached for her laptop and began to type up something that had to be more convincing than any essay she had ever written. It would make anyone say "yes." Wren thought of her lawyer parents as she typed what she knew they dealt with all the time, something she knew they would have to respect: a contract.

Chapter 3

"Are you dumb?"

Wren rolled her eyes. "Ro, why do you doubt me?" she spoke into her phone.

Their video chat had glitched for a moment and fixed itself, matching Rohit's movements.

"Because you sometimes have crazy ideas that I never understand."

"I won't get you into trouble," Wren said, organizing her papers into folders.

He scoffed.

"Ro, have I ever gotten you in trouble?"

He let out a sigh and a simple "no."

"I'm sending you a copy of the contract right now. It should cover everything, but feel free to edit and add anything, Mr. Valedictorian."

There was a long pause before Rohit drew a breath. "Stop that."

"Stop wha—"

"I know that we don't get jealous over this kind of stuff, but I can tell it's been bothering you that I got valedictorian. You have to know that nothing is going to change the fact they awarded me over you." The panicked realization of his comment flashed in Rohit's dark eyes. He knew instantly that he had taken a step too far, that his words just tumbled out of his mouth, and he couldn't figure out how to put them back in without Wren noticing.

"That was a dick move," Wren muttered, a little too loud to be under her breath. The fact that he had just gotten top of the class was like the A– she got in AP Economics. It had ticked her off a little, but she had tried to live with it. Rohit stared at her through the screen but kept dropping his eyes to avoid her gaze. "I'm not jealous of you. Get a hold of your ego, Ro. I'm fine. Actually, better than fine. I'm great, and I don't mind the fact that my best friend will be standing right next to me at graduation, no matter who got what position. So just drop it, Ro, because you're sounding like a grade A asshole."

There was a long pause before Rohit finally spoke up. "I'm sorry," he muttered before a grin grew across his face. "But at least I get an A for being an asshole."

Wren's eyes rolled in the way they always did, fueled with sarcasm. Rohit and Wren had their fair share of fights, but this was not one of them.

Another two hours rolled by in conversation before Rohit finally asked Wren what her plan was when she presented her parents with the contract she formulated.

"I think I'm going to tell them tonight."

"Tonight?" Rohit gulped.

"You always do this, Ro. You just gotta rip the Band-Aid off. You always procrastinate telling your parents stuff."

"That's because I would like to avoid getting my ass kicked for as long as possible before disappointing my parents," he countered.

"No one is getting their ass kicked, Ro. You don't have to tell your parents yet. We'll see how things play out with mine first, and then I'll report back."

"You're the best, Wren," Rohit said, with his whole heart in it.

"I know. That's why you love me." She smiled back at him and hung up.

***

Wren descended the stairs with two copies of the contract she formulated in folders for both her parents. They were in the back of the house at the dining room table, separated by a fresh pot of coffee and stacks of papers, worn down from a long day's work. Their eyes barely lifted at Wren's presence.

"Do you think you guys could use a break?" Wren spoke with the hope imminent in her voice.

"Sure," her father replied, taking off his glasses, eager for any distraction from the mountain of work before them. Her mother took a long glance at her work, but eventually put her papers to the side to focus on her daughter.

Wren tossed a folder in front of her mother and another in front of her father and said, "I want to sneak out." Her parent's faces contorted in pure confusion only to open their folders to find clearly organized and concise notes about the agreement she had bestowed before them. They read for a couple minutes, stealing glances at their daughter, and making shocked eye contact at certain sections of the page. Her father looked up and winked at his daughter, signing the forms quickly, but her mother clutched to it like the contract had been used on her as a weapon.

"Michael, how could you sign it so easily?" Wren's mother hissed. She was always the more stern one, the one in charge, the drill sergeant.

"What? Vanessa, she's seventeen years old, eighteen in a few months, and she's a good girl. She never does anything bad—"

"And this agreement permits her to make rash decisions."

Wren got her interrupting habit from her mother.

"Rash decisions? Vanessa, she hasn't done a bad thing in her life. What type of rash decisions could she possibly make?" he asked, trying to mask a chuckle in his voice.

"Yeah, Mom. It's not like I'm going to kill somebody."

Her mother merely glared at her with intense eyes. She never found Wren's sarcasm amusing.

"Wren, honey. Go upstairs. We'll talk to you about this later," her dad instructed kindly. Wren could always rely on her father, because when Ro wasn't around, he was her best friend.

Wren skipped a single step while going upstairs and realized that this was nothing to get happy about so soon.

They hadn't said yes... yet. She could be very persuasive when she wanted to be. This would take longer than usual, but it was okay for her since she was only a senior for two more months. Her mom would take some time to figure things out, but it would never take too long. This was a minor victory that Rohit would want to hear about.

Wren: mom's still on the fence about it but dad signed it almost immediately

Rohit: LMK when both your parents are on board. I'm getting sick to my stomach just thinking ab this

Wren rolled her eyes. Rohit could be such a wimp sometimes, even through text when he had the chance to mask his true feelings. She knew that it would take an annoyingly long time to get Rohit to enjoy their night out, but it would be worth it for both of them. They would get to let loose and just enjoy the time that they didn't have to act like themselves.

Wren hopped in the shower, undoing her long braids and letting her chestnut hair fall down past her shoulder blades. She turned the water almost all the way to the left, where it was borderline boiling, and let the steam roll off her back. She let out an exasperated sigh. Her body felt drained after her mother's words. Vanessa Clements was always the one who cracked the whip, not that there was much of a whip to crack with her daughter. Wren always behaved, but if you asked the woman, she would be tempted to admit that her daughter was a nuisance.

Wren looked down at her upper thigh. A scratch, nearly healed, lay cleanly across her rosy skin. Wren sometimes wondered why she didn't take a razor and simply cut and cut and cut until her whole left leg was gone. Maybe she didn't want to admit that she was that damaged. Maybe she didn't want to admit that she cared about her mother's opinion of her that much.

Wren tried extremely hard to not let people see the other side of her. She liked being wonderfully complicated, but she hated that the one person she should feel the closest to still hasn't bothered to see past her outer layer. The cut was almost entirely healed, but she still raised her razor and slit the same line of skin, letting just the tiniest drops spill out and swirl at the bottom of the shower. Within seconds, they were drowned and pulled down the drain, never to be looked at again.

Wren felt the slightest bit of a release. That was all she needed—to feel something.

Chapter 4

———

The next morning, Wren woke up to an alarm of the local radio station.

It was five thirty in the morning, and the radio show host was advertising a new game on full blast. Wren groaned, but she got up to go through all her daily rituals. Take out her retainer, brush her teeth, use the bathroom, change into leggings and a sports bra, and finally, go for a run.

She clicked on her playlist and then she was off to run her daily three-mile morning run, the only thing to properly wake her up. When the first mile went by in a blink, Wren decided to unplug, letting her headphones fall to her side. Just at the end of Church Street, an empty sea of grass laid perfectly undisturbed. Where the sun finally started to peak out behind the cloudiness of the morning, there was the smallest patch warm from the sunshine. Wren darted to it and planted her face in the patch of sun and the rest of her body in the shadow of morning dew covered grass. She smiled like a blissful child without a care in the world.

If only she didn't have a care in the world.

There are two sides to everyone...

She felt her tired eyes droop and close out the world around her as the warmth intensified, almost infinite. Wren stopped to listen to the wind travel through the trees and hear the chirping of the birds. In this moment, she felt so close to earth that no grades, no choices, no opinions, no nothing mattered in the world, except for her in this tiny bed of grass. She wanted to believe that the sunshine wanted her as much as she wanted it, but she was afraid that not even the brightest thing in the world could want her.

With that thought, she got up with a force so frozen it could have turned day into night, and she continued to run another two miles. She could have run longer; in fact, she wanted to. She wanted to feel what it would be like to have no air in your body, to have the insides scream out for help. But time was going by fast, and she still had the whole day ahead of her. *Maybe next time*, she thought.

***

With a simple turn of a key through her back door, Wren found her mother waiting for her at the kitchen island, chin deep in a hot black coffee. Wren's mother stood at five-foot eight, three inches shy of her husband and towering three massive inches above her daughter. Her face started to wrinkle during her early twenties and only continued to grow years after. Nothing a little airbrushing couldn't solve.

Wren had always advised her mother to not engage in such floozy affairs, yet her mother persisted, claiming that a fresh face was always the fiercest in court.

Her auburn hair was graying at the tips again, she would retouch them later this week. She only ever wore pant-suits, and her briefcase always had a seat at the table. She was two years away from fifty, but Wren swore her mother had the personality of an elderly woman who was bitter that her life and body were slowly deteriorating before her very eyes.

"Wren," her mother started sternly as Wren grabbed a bottle of water from the fridge. The only thing that separated them was a set of papers. Wren's papers. Not just the contract, but report cards, medical reports, awards, letters of recommendation, acceptance letters—everything. Wren's whole life was sitting there on the table.

Wren took a gulp of water before asking, "What is all this?"

Vanessa Clements cleared her throat before she began. "Your father and I were discussing the terms of your contract last night. And it's not right."

"Is it in the wrong format?"

"No, Wren, it's not that. Take a look at everything on this table. Look at these awards."

Wren's eyes scanned over the table. They flicked from paper to transcript to letter. They all glowed with accomplishment. Wren looked back up to make eye contact with her mother only to break it immediately before her mother started to speak.

"It's you," she said, in a taunting manner. "Imagine if I were to throw all of these out."

Wren's eyes could have popped out of her sockets. Her mother smirked, and Wren hated herself for giving her mother the slightest bit of satisfaction.

"Yes. That is exactly what you are doing if this 'sneaking out' stunt gets out of hand. If you mess up, your reputation goes down the drain. Is it really that worth it? You're so close to the end of high school."

Wren felt a knot in her stomach grow. It tightened more and more, so much she thought she might implode. Her eyes stung, but something else hurt her even more: the thought of not being able to spend this one night actually trying to find herself. She already knew who she was, but she wanted to get to know the person she could have been, given the circumstances. And just like that, the knot loosened just a little.

"I know what you're trying to do, Mom. I respect it, and I respect you. I just think... no, I *know* this is something I need to do. And when do I ever mess up?" Wren regretted the question the minute she asked it. She knew her mother could come up with a list of things that didn't meet her standards.

With one reluctant movement, Vanessa Clements signed on the dotted line. Wren wished she could have captured the moment on video. The moment her mother signed away her ownership over Wren's freedom for one whole night.

Wren showered and got ready for school as quickly as she could. Her hand was trembling with excitement, brushing mascara onto her eyelashes and doing her hair in a half up-half down. She put on a cute blouse paired with some blue jeans, already embracing the giddiness of being a normal teenager. As soon as she was ready, she hopped in her car and zoomed to the parking lot, radiating nerves and anticipation. She couldn't wait to see Rohit's face when she would present him with her parent's approval. She envisioned it the entire way there, squealing to herself. Nothing but adrenaline pumping in her veins.

***

Rohit's mornings were always the same. He woke up at six thirty in the morning, took a shower, and prayed in his family's Hindu temple at home.

"Pray for good grades," his mother instructed him as she nodded to the textbooks that were blessed by God before them.

"Mom, I already have good grades. Report cards came out already. Remember?" Rohit whined.

"Hey!" she yelled, sliding off her slipper into her hand and waving it in the air. "Don't talk back! They'll think you're ungrateful," she threatened, eyeing the statues of Hindu gods with mercy in her eyes. "Sorry, bolo!" she commanded in Hindi.

"I'm sorry."

"Not to me, Rohit!"

Rohit shifted his direction to face the temple. He pressed his hands together in front of his chest, closed his eyes, and said, "I am so sorry. Thank you for everything you've done for me." And then he knelt with his head to the ground for a minute, thinking *Please don't punish me for my behavior,* reaching his right hand toward the shrine, and touching it back to his forehead.

"Good. Now you better not behave like this when you go to Brown, Rohit. I mean it! You can't say bad things or forget to pray."

"I know, Mom." Rohit resisted the urge to roll his eyes. It's not like it was his hard work that got him his spot in Brown. No, it was all just the work of the gods. *Sorry,* he thought, glancing back at the Hindu figures before him.

"Did you look into taking some summer classes to get ahead?" Rohit's father asked, glasses foggy over his morning cup of coffee.

Rohit picked himself up from the floor and straightened out his clothes. He passed the mantle place where his parents had their own shrine to their kids—photos of him and his sister, Ria, accomplishing various things stacked upon each other. It was always a major conversation point between guests, and the Kumar parents had intentionally positioned it that way.

Rohit rolled his eyes every time he saw it. There's nothing wrong with showing off if you're humble about it, but his parents were anything but humble. He supposed that it wasn't their fault; it was simply how they were raised. Indian people were always trying to one up each other.

He took a seat next to his dad at the table and reached for the coffee pot.

"Rohit, you know the rules," his mother chided, placing a tall glass of milk before him instead. "It'll stunt your growth."

"Mom, I'm eighteen and already five-foot eleven. I'm past the age of growth spirts." Rohit sighed, powerless. He was having this same argument every day, and if he hadn't been getting coffee with Wren since sophomore year he would have never known what the bitter energy burst tasted like.

"Listen to your mother," Mr. Kumar commanded behind his morning newspaper. Suddenly, he put it down, eyes traveling all over his son. "What are you wearing?"

"Just a T-shirt and shorts," Rohit mumbled before he gulped down his glass of milk.

"Are you going to school or to a fashion show?" his mother barked as her son stood up quickly, tossing his backpack over his shoulder.

"Gotta go. Bye, love you!" Rohit shouted on his way to the door.

"Make sure to look into taking summer classes!" his father shouted after him before the door closed on Rohit's way out.

He hopped on the bus and put his headphones in, turning on his playlist to drown out the noisy bus conversation. The lyrics of "The Middle" by Jimmy Eat World traveled through his ears as he started thinking about how nice it will be to go to college and be independent. He couldn't wait to get away from his parent's incessant nagging and commands.

***

With the contract in one hand, Wren had a new spring in her step when she made her way to school. She made it to homeroom just before the bell and slapped the contract on Rohit's desk. He studied it, and when his eyes found the signatures, his whole body language shifted with eagerness. He looked at her with a dazed look in his eyes. "How *do* you do it?"

"I know. I'm just that amazing." Wren laughed sarcastically. She was just relieved she had the opportunity to do this, not just for her, but for Rohit.

"So what's the next step?" he questioned, with a new grin on his face. His face mirrored a child's, excited to be doing something they know they shouldn't.

"We get the others." Wren smirked, riding the high from her accomplishment.

She had a really good feeling about this. She could tell that she was going to like this new Wren. That she would like the taste of this new forbidden life.

Rohit took care of recruiting Tyler Harrison. He walked up to him in AP calculus and simply slid him a $100 bill and asked Tyler to go to his dealer and get some of his best stuff. Tyler didn't believe it at first. He thought the whole thing was a set up, but Rohit assured him that he wouldn't want to be seen buying drugs with Brown on the line. It was that simple—Tyler was in. Then there was Mia Young, who took a little more convincing.

"So, this is just because my boyfriend works at the liquor store and you need stuff?" she half asked, rolling her eyes.

People always came to her for stuff like that. *Hey Mia, can your boyfriend hook us up?* never, *Hey Mia, how are you doing?* Sometimes she hated her tie to her boyfriend's job, but she loved him. He had graduated two years before and was taking night classes to get his degree at a discount. Some people called him a deadbeat, but Mia knew better than that. He was kind and just took a while to get his life together. But she liked that about him.

He was like her. Just trying to live life, be happy, and not put up with any bullshit. They had spent Saturday mornings in his apartment watching reruns of *I Love Lucy* and dancing around his kitchen to old records. She took tons of photos of him. They had amazing sex. They enjoyed each others' company.

And then everyone had to come and ruin it the second people started recognizing him at the liquor store and he stopped carding people. Not that anyone in their town really cared, but it was still a nuisance nevertheless. It was just another thing that reminded Mia that she was dating an older man who might think that her antics were childish.

Wren instantly regretted her honest approach, realizing too deep into the conversation that her intentions had been a little too obvious.

"No," Wren started, "it's actually an excuse to, umm… hang out with you."

This was a tactic she had learned in a summer program for psychology. It wasn't exactly rocket science, but Wren knew that some people just needed to hear what they wanted to, and most of the time that revolved around flattery. People loved to talk about themselves, it was a clear fact.

"Hang out with me? We've spoken for maybe five minutes throughout all of high school."

Rohit didn't miss a beat. He continued with, "We always thought *you* didn't like us, but we wanted to give trying to be friends with you a shot before we all graduate. Hey, we just want to have fun, that's all." Rohit finished with raising his hands in the air in an honest surrender.

She considered this for a moment and then slammed her locker shut. She bit a fingernail while eyeing Rohit and Wren up and down. If it were Wren asking by herself, Mia surely would have declined, but Rohit was always better with girls than her. With a heavy breath, she nodded and gave Rohit her phone number. And with that, she took off to her class.

"Ro, I have no clue how I would be able to get this done without you." Wren punched his shoulder softly.

"Well, you better figure it out, because we have lunch next and so does Sammy, Derek, and Valerie. We gotta split up if we wanna cover more ground," Rohit pointed out.

"Okay. I'll handle Sammy and Valerie. They seem to be some of the only girls in this school who don't hate me. You get Derek."

With a nod, the pair split and went out in search of their marks. Wren started to feel a little nervous, but she had a plan. It was no secret that people rolled their eyes at her when her hand shot up in class or tried to ignore her when she talked sometimes, but these girls didn't mind. It was almost like they understood Wren for the way she was, without even talking to her. That's what made her approach them with slightly more confidence than what she would normally have. She saw Valerie first and waved her way. Valerie beckoned for her to come over and sit next to her at her table.

Valerie Scott was always a pleasure to talk to. She was one of those girls that parents compare you to, not for her grades or for anything academic at all, but for being involved in the community and having people skills unlike anyone else. Not to mention, she always came to school perfectly made up. In such a way, she never failed to make the majority of the student body stare in awe, smile, and wonder what it would be like to marry her. She radiated pure happiness.

The great thing about Valerie, though, was that she was incredibly humble about it all. She was so comfortable with people that she called nearly everyone she met "babe." It was her token of charm, and for some reason no one was ever bothered by it. Rohit had once mentioned to Wren a few months ago that he thought Valerie Scott was just about the greatest human god had dropped on earth, and Wren knew that Valerie, someone who thought she wasn't anything special, would be happy to hear that.

"Wren!" She squealed, moving her lunch away from where Wren was about to sit. "How are you, babe?"

"I'm great, Valerie. How are you?"

"Pretty good. I haven't seen you since we volunteered to clean up the park."

"Well, yeah. I've been pretty busy since then."

It came out with an unintended rudeness. A small silence passed. Valerie's smile drifted down a tiny bit as she realized Wren wasn't going to add on anything else to her comment. The good thing about Valerie was that she knew when people were being rude and when they were being awkward, and she had known Wren long enough to know that this was one of her awkward moments.

There are two sides to everyone...

"I bet! It's not easy getting into UPenn. I'm sure your schedule has been packed!" Valerie complimented with a genuine smile. It was that smile that had almost all of the school either wishing they could either date Valerie or be Valerie. She was living, breathing proof of people wanting to change for the better. And that made Wren smile genuinely too, because she was going to feed off of Valerie's energy and change for the better too.

"Actually, I do have some free time coming up, now that you mention it. What if I told you that I was going to sneak out one night and I wanted you to come with me?"

"What? Me?"

"No, not just you. Rohit, Mia, Tyler, and hopefully a few other people. Just to go around town and have one super fun night."

"What type of fun?" Valerie raised her eyebrows before taking a sip of her water.

Wren wasn't hurt by this question. She was well aware that people thought her idea of fun was solving differential equations. Which before it was, but she wanted more for that night.

"I don't know. Maybe get drunk, go to a party. If you come with a bunch of your famous dares, it'll be guaranteed to be an epic night." Wren was really trying to sell it. She wanted Valerie there a little bit more than the others, because Valerie knew how to bridge the gap. She could move past awkward moments, and the night would never be dull if she was there.

"Wow, Wren. I didn't know you and Rohit would be up for one of my dares, let alone sneaking out."

It was no secret that Valerie's dares were dangerously bold, but they always made for the best stories, which is why Wren and Rohit wanted her there so badly.

"We are. And I think Rohit would be especially happy if you came." Wren winked.

"What do you mean?" Valerie's face flushed with tingly heat. She tucked one of her perfect locks of hair behind one of her perfect ears.

"He thinks you're pretty great. And I don't think he would mind trying to get to know you a little more." Wren knew her answer from the growing smile on her face. For once it was so easy for Wren to speak "girl" that she thought for a second that talking to other people might not be so incredibly difficult.

"Okay. I'll be there. Text me."

Wren's chest filled with warmth at her words. It was all coming together. Wren nodded as she got up and caught sight of Rohit, who was a few tables over. He was smiling while talking to Derek.

"Dude, your art is amazing," Rohit complimented him, holding up his phone to scroll through Derek's Instagram feed.

"Thanks, man." Derek flashed a smile back. He had his back to his friends, who were all in deep conversation. "I don't always do street art. I also started to do some on canvas. I'm actually trying to get into this elite art program."

"That's awesome. I'd love to see your work in action," Rohit suggested.

"Huh?"

"Look, I could really use your help..." Rohit met Wren's glance for a second and then caught something in the corner of his eye. He diverted his attention across the cafeteria to Sammy Rodriguez, who was leaving to head to the bathroom.

Wren didn't miss a beat. Her footfalls matched the pattern of Sammy's heading into the bathroom past the cafeteria. There was a perfectly fine bathroom right outside the cafeteria. Why had she gone all the way down the hall? Wren added ample space between her and her mark, avoiding eye contact and any sign that she had been following Sammy.

Wren saw Sammy's chocolate hair get tossed up in a lopsided pony as she ducked her whole body behind the door of the bathroom. The door shut with a loud clatter and the echo dared Wren to not follow her. But then again, Wren's new thing was breaking the rules. With a sigh and a drop in her shoulders, Wren darted into the bathroom, perfectly aware of why Sammy had chosen this particular bathroom.

Sammy's eyes watered with the memories of the kickback she went to the night before. Everyone was plastered, just like she was. They had teased her about being a lightweight, unable to handle too much liquor. If only they knew... That morning, Sammy had eaten the big breakfast her mother had made her. She treated her hangover with eggs and toast and even a pancake. She washed it all down with an orange juice and coffee. She would see them all again soon, flushing away her latest disappointment.

Wren waited as quietly as she could, careful not to scare Sammy off. She rested by the sinks, trying to tune out the noise until Sammy unlocked the door of her stall, wiping her lips and blinking back tears in her eyes. The hazel in Sammy's glassy eyes grew darker as the image of Wren standing before her grew clearer.

"Wren... Uh, I didn't think anyone else was in here... I just..." Sammy tried to explain herself and gave up halfway, resorting to washing her hands and rinsing out her mouth.

Wren touched the edge of her elbow as a peace offering. "You don't have to explain."

Sammy fell silent. She was now fixing her hair and pulling her bra straps closer to her clavicle, moving the shirtsleeves off her shoulders.

Wren tried again. "Do you wanna talk about it?"

Sammy rolled her eyes, "Cut the crap, Wren. What do you care?" Her voice was soft, but her words were like daggers.

Wren understood that she had tread on private ground. She was not meant to know about *this* Sammy. No one was. Those words felt like rubbing salt in a wound. Sammy took notice to the hurt in Wren's eyes and the step back that she took. Sammy wanted to take those words back for a second, but decided that this wasn't Perfect Wren's problem to deal with. It was hers. Wren seemed to know everything about everything, but this was not her business. If her secret had gotten out, everything would be over. She was not going to let a little purging ruin her. "Can you please keep this to yourself? I just don't want people knowing. You know, I have a reputation."

"I get it," Wren heard herself saying. As Sammy stepped closer toward the door, Wren's voice took on a

There are two sides to everyone...

mind of its own. "More than you think." Sammy stopped abruptly and turned her head, her eyes fixing in on a frozen Wren.

"You? You have an eating disorder? Richmond High's pride and joy Wren with the good grades and killer extracurriculars?"

Wren felt a stab of fear. She was washed over with the feeling of nakedness, and a spotlight had been drawn directly to every flaw she'd ever had. "No, not an eating disorder specifically." Wren couldn't believe her own conscience. It was betraying itself, programmed to self-destruct. There was no off switch; it just kept going like an uncontrollable gear. "Lock the door," she told Sammy before tears began to stream down her face. They were hot and stung with regret and relief all at once.

"Wren, what the hell are you talking about? Are you okay?"

"I promise not to tell if you promise not to," Wren blurted.

"About what?" Sammy half shouted. Her volume had overpowered their level of secrecy, so she whispered it again, turning a head even though the door was locked and there was no chance anyone else was getting in.

Wren let out a heavy sigh that didn't make her feel any better than the vulnerable state she had set up for herself. She lifted her shirt hem and tugged down at the belt loop of her pants to reveal four slits. One was scarred, two were healing, and the other was freshly cut. Sammy's eyes widened, and in that moment Wren knew there was no turning back. She let go of her shirt and slid to the bathroom floor with tears brimming over her sunken lids.

She was exhausted, upset, uptight, driven, and lonely all at once. It was too much for her. In that moment where she was able to let somebody in, Wren felt a bigger release than she had ever felt with the single movement of a blade. She half expected Sammy to leave her there, cracked and vulnerable on the bathroom floor, but she joined her and held her hand in understanding. When Wren was done, she could hardly look Sammy in the eyes. Wren was disgusted with herself.

"Why do you do it?"

"Why do you purge?"

"You want the easy answer or the complex answer?" Sammy sighed, painfully liberated.

It shocked Wren to know that in that moment, the person she connected to the most was Sammy Rodriguez, the crazy party girl who had the high school reputation of an extremely experienced college student.

"Let's hear them both."

Sammy unfolded her legs and drew them close to her chest. "The simple answer is that I hate my body. The other one is that—"

"It's a release." Wren found herself filling in the blank. And with that, Sammy looked into Wren's eyes and knew the two of them were never really that different. It meant neither of them felt so alone anymore, and that meant the world.

"Yeah." Sammy breathed. "You too, huh?"

Wren felt her head nod. "There's a lot of pressure to be perfect all the time. Sometimes you just need to get away and feel *something*... anything."

Sammy nodded in understanding. The two were the same. For a moment, Wren had forgotten all about the contract and about sneaking out. And even though Sammy was just another person to string along in her plan, she had been grateful to have connected with her like this because it meant that their night out wouldn't be a night out with strangers, but with people she connected with. It brought the faintest smile to her face.

"What?"

"Being perfect sucks, and I'm just now understanding it."

Sammy laughed a sigh. "Yeah. You gotta get out somehow."

"I know," Wren started, carefully picking her next words out as to transition into the topic of their night out without sounding like that was all that Sammy was for. "Rohit and I were talking about that a lot over the weekend, and we decided that the best way to experience *not* being perfect is to break the rules and sneak out one night."

"And do what?" Sammy chuckled, at first not believing in Wren's plan.

"Anything, really. But we can't do it alone. We know a lot of things, but not about this stuff. So would you maybe want to come with us? Make sure that we actually get the full experience?" Wren asked, convincing her.

Sammy didn't have to think hard about it. She saw something in Wren that a lot of people couldn't. She saw the human side of Wren, which was a side no one else bothered to get to know. People always assumed she was more robot than human, but Sammy never listened to them. She was raised to give people the benefit of the doubt, and through the years she never listened to what people would say about Wren.

"So it's just us three?" Sammy smiled, offering Wren a hand, raising her up off of the ground.

"Well, actually, no. We also recruited Valerie, Derek, Mia, and Tyler. We want every experience we missed out on for one, wild night."

"Sounds like you're starting to learn something about a proper release." Sammy smiled, her hand on the door-knob. "Text me the details."

Sammy gave Wren's shoulder a reassuring squeeze before saying goodbye and leaving Wren all alone again.

Chapter 5

———

Wren had taken time to wrangle her emotions after what happened in the bathroom. She needed to be her normal self if she wanted to get Asa on board. He was the last one left, and as Wren made her way to Econ she made sure to use their chemistry to her advantage.

She flashed Asa a shy smile before taking her seat behind his desk. The woodsy scent of Old Spice lingered around him, causing Wren's heart to skip a beat. She pulled her pencil and notebook out, but she caught herself staring at his broad shoulders and the back of his neck instead of at the board. Tiny, dark chocolate curls were trimmed neatly above his perfectly coffee colored skin.

She often got lost in him. And he, the same.

Wren almost didn't notice a dull Mr. Alcott writing the day's lesson plans on the white board. He stood with a curved posture, uncomfortable in his change in attire. He wore a new button down and had his hair gelled instead of his usual minimal effort of a worn-out polo tucked into khakis.

"Yo, Mr. Alcott. Got a date or something?" someone from the back of the classroom whispered. Snickers and turning heads followed.

"I thought he hated everyone since his nasty divorce," another whisper followed.

"That would explain why I'm getting a C in this dumb class," someone from the right corner scoffed.

"Good for him if he does have a date," Asa whispered to Wren. "Everyone deserves someone to make them happy. Even him."

"I know you all are done with the AP exam," Mr. Alcott finally spoke up in his usual monotone. "But here's some work for you all to do. Problems due at the end of class or it's homework for half credit."

The class filled with groans and angry flipping of pages. Desks screeched against the linoleum floor, students scooting closer together to work on the long list of problems. Asa routinely turned his desk to face a glowing Wren. Although she hated Mr. Alcott and that A- that she had been given, she was grateful for his seating chart. Asa sat so close to her that she feared her body would explode from excitement.

Asa closed the space between him and Wren to ask her a question. The scent of her lavender shampoo made his stomach do flips. Wren reverted her eyes from the page as she saw his fingertips graze the side of her desk. Her cheeks flushed just to look at him.

"This isn't making any sense to me." He laughed nervously. His knee brushed against hers and simply laid there, eager.

Wren bit her lip, trying to hide a smile. "No worries." It was charming how shy he was to ask for help, and how brave he was to ask for *her* help. He would ask her about everything, and she had to admit to herself that she liked the attention.

The next time they looked up at the clock nearly twenty minutes had passed. "Cool. I get it now." Asa smiled back, and Wren could feel herself melting. He turned his desk back around, unsure of what to say next, and to his surprise, he felt Wren tap his shoulder.

"Bear with me. This is going to sound crazy." She bit her lip.

"I love crazy," Asa found himself saying, not entirely sure that was true.

"No, you don't." Wren smirked.

"What can I say? There's a lot you don't know about me."

An exaggerated scoff sounded from the corner. It was Stella Lu. Her voice triggered an immediate eye roll from Wren. Stella was always trying to get under Wren's skin. It was clear that Stella had wanted everything Wren had: the grades, the life, and even being best friends with Rohit. So Stella got into the habit of trying to beat Wren for salutatorian. Anytime Stella got a 96 percent, Wren would somehow pull through with a 98 percent.

"Can you guys stop flirting so loudly? Some of us are trying to get some work done." She groaned.

"Don't you mean trying too hard, Stella?" Wren fired back.

"Careful, Wren. If you lose focus, you might find that I'll end up on top," she taunted, eyeing Wren like a piece of meat.

Wren's mind went back to all-nighters in the library, overly preparing for exams to ensure that Stella would not beat her. She could not afford to disappoint her parents in another way. She succeeded in beating Stella, but that didn't stop Stella from threatening her as if she had some sort of trick up her sleeve. Wren tried her best to ignore Stella and her ego. But somehow Wren's fingers grazed her upper thigh, feeling where her exposed flesh was sliced the night before. She pulled her finger back fast enough and told herself that Stella was just jealous. *Relax. No need to keep cutting.*

"Hey," Asa whispered, taking a leap by squeezing Wren's wrist. "Ignore her."

Wren came to her senses the second she felt his skin on hers. "Right." She shook her head. "What was I saying?"

"Something crazy." Asa smiled.

"Right, something crazy."

Stella rolled her eyes, got out of her seat, and marched her way to the front of the classroom to turn in the assignment. She started a discussion with Mr. Alcott, and Wren had to only assume she was begging him for extra credit. Just one last "fuck you" before they all left for good.

"So, Ro and I had this idea..." Wren began.

From the moment the plan left her lips she knew that Asa would have agreed to go with her, no matter what. Hell, he would have even gone with her to go dumpster diving if she asked him. He just wanted to be with her, even if craziness was what she wanted. Even so, he hoped by the end of the night, she'd see she didn't need any of that.

He liked Wren because the thing that mattered most to her was working hard. She wasn't like their classmates who went to parties and drank too much. She was herself all the time, and to him she didn't need to adopt that teenage rule-breaking fantasy.

But it was the craziness she craved, so Asa agreed to go with her. No questions asked.

Chapter 6

———

Rohit had a nervous grin slapped across his face when he met up with Wren at the end of the day.

He couldn't believe that they had gotten everyone on board with the plan. He always knew Wren was determined, but it was always a grade that kept her motivated. He was both scared and amused at the fact that this was truly what she wanted.

"We did it!" she squealed, giving him a hug.

Rohit's hands lingered longer against her back, hoping to hold her just for a moment more. "I can't imagine that Asa needed too much convincing." He smiled through the pain.

"Oh, stop. He was clearly interested in sneaking out as well." Wren shoved his shoulder hard.

"He's clearly interested in you." He winked. "And look who can't stop blushing," he pointed out, hoping to shame her out of falling for the wrong guy. The guy who was naturally intelligent and was fine with it. The guy who decided not to push himself the way Wren and Rohit did, but enjoy where he was. And where he was at was a great place to be if it meant Wren was in it.

"He's a good guy, that's all. And he's *normal!*" Wren pointed out, trying to justify her point. "I deserve this. *We* deserve this. We've worked so hard, and now we get to have some fun."

"Well if my parents say no to this, the whole plan will go to shit," Rohit pointed out, trying to move on from his thoughts.

"You think they'll say no? Have you forgotten who's doing the convincing? Ro, I take it as an insult that you don't believe in me."

Rohit bumped her shoulder. "Of course I believe in you." His mind drowned in thoughts of how the night would go if they actually managed to sneak out. What would they do? Would he finally tell Wren that sometimes he thought they could be more? Would he be happy doing this? He just hoped that whatever it was that Wren was looking for, he would find it too.

The pair made their way to Wren's car in the school parking lot. Wren drove a dark green Mini Cooper that her parents got her for her sixteenth birthday. Her mother didn't want to get her anything at all that year, or any year, frankly, but her father insisted as a reward for many years of hard work.

"I literally can't wait, Ro!" Wren squealed as the pair buckled their seatbelts and got ready to drive home. "What do you think pot tastes like?"

"The way it smells." Rohit snorted. "Ugh, it's gonna be so bad."

"Well, get used to it, Ro. Because in college you might be a lot diff—"

Out of nowhere, a light green Volkswagen bug almost took off Wren's entire fender. Fear and relief washed over her body as they were six inches from a serious trip to the hospital, but amidst that, a fiery fury exploded as she rolled down her window to scream at the driver.

The driver's window came down, revealing a girl with charcoal hair, fair skin, and almond eyes with a signature death glare. Stella Lu. It came as no surprise to Wren that it was her. Wren often called her car a horrific Ted Bundy style vehicle, and it was too recognizable at Richmond High.

"You fucking psycho! Learn how to fucking drive!" screamed Wren, hoping that Stella would break down in tears apologizing and begging for forgiveness.

Stella merely put on a pair of sunglasses, looked back at Wren, who was still screaming blasphemous words at her, and stuck her middle finger out the window before driving off completely unfazed.

"That bitch has been trying to kill me for years," Wren found herself saying. "Fucking bitch."

"Relax. We survived." Rohit always tried to give Stella Lu the benefit of the doubt. He figured he would be just like her if he didn't have a best friend like Wren.

"Relax? I wouldn't have an arrhythmia right now if that girl just took her car and drove herself off the face of the earth."

"You know that's not possible. Even if the world was flat and you could fall off the face of the earth, you wouldn't be able to get rid of her that easily."

After spending the entire trip home ranting about Stella, Wren finally pulled into her driveway. Within seconds they were both racing up to her room, mostly out of habit. Rohit was going to need a lot of courage to pull this off, and he would most definitely need his partner in crime by his side.

"We need to win my parents over. Really butter them up before we dump this news in front of them."

"Dinner?" Wren suggested.

Wren and Rohit almost always thought the same things, and that's what made them a perfect pair. That is, when Wren didn't come up with crazy ideas. Rohit's stomach gurgled with anxiety. He never asked his parents for much, but this seemed almost like he was asking to be emancipated. But he was eighteen. He was an adult. He was capable of making his own decisions, though his Indian heritage thought otherwise. It was typical for Indian children to please their traditional parents. Actually, it was expected of them.

They grew up like careers in *The Hunger Games*. They trained to be the best of the best, and every flawless grade they got boosted them further in the competition. They studied for the SAT starting in seventh grade. They learned to be good at sports and musical instruments and how to be people pleasers. Indian children were groomed to be picture perfect, and the cycle would continue when they had kids.

Rohit was happy to be part of that cycle. He was proud to be Indian, though he tried to be more humble about his accomplishments. He could make his family proud and build a name for himself, and ultimately become successful. Wren could do the same, so it truly perplexed him that she was such an advocate for sneaking out. But when Wren set her mind to something, she made it a point to achieve her goals. If he fought against the idea, it would only push her harder. He often just agreed with her because it was the easier option. She was wonderfully thick headed like that.

Thanks to a busy year of hard work and summer quickly approaching, Wren and Rohit were happy to not have homework to do anymore. There were no tests, there were no projects; all they had was time to hang out together. Rohit sometimes felt like he was wasting the time he was given. He could be learning JavaScript or Mandarin or the guitar (something his parents thought less of). But he found himself spending his extra time with Wren, having either deep discussions on life or watching a new movie.

***

After preparing a dinner of vegetarian lasagna, a bottle of wine, and chocolate cake, Wren and Rohit waited for their parents by watching the famous blockbuster movies they missed out on. They watched *Knives Out* and were deep in discussion. Rohit always preferred something sci-fi and dystopian, while Wren always preferred crime and action. The jump scares and exhilarating suspense fed into her minor obsession, but it was the theories that kept her hooked. She supposed that this was because she was the daughter of two successful lawyers and she was always trained to think about what people want to believe versus what actually happened. She knew a case could easily be built against anyone, and detectives often solved the case based on who has the most amount of evidence behind the crime. But Wren knew this was what was wrong with law enforcement. She knew there is more to people than what meets the eye.

Wren chuckled as she listened to Detective Blanc go on about the "donut" in the case. Rohit looked over at her with a grin and heat rising in his cheeks, as if that laugh was music to his ears. He tried to hide it. *It's for the better,* he thought to himself.

"There's no way in hell Marta did it."

"She confessed," Rohit pointed out.

"You would make a shitty detective. Look at her. She's good."

"Good people can kill too."

"Maybe, but not here. I think it was Ransom."

"Why?"

"He's always lurking in the back. And now all of a sudden he's interested in Marta?"

"Maybe they were both in on it."

"She wouldn't throw her life away for him. She's too smart."

Sure enough, Wren was right. The last twenty minutes showed Detective Blanc proving just that: Ransom committed the crime and framed Marta. She lived a happy life after, away from the drama. It was a life she deserved, and that brought a warm smile to Wren's face.

"Okay, you got me."

"Why are you not surprised?" Wren laughed.

Just then the front door clicked open, and both Wren and Rohit's parents shuffled in, deep in conversation. Wren and Rohit stood up and quickly reheated the lasagna and filled the glasses with wine.

"Amma, Appa, take a seat." Rohit gestured, pulling out two chairs.

"What do you want, Beta?" His mom asked, not missing a beat. "You only call us Amma and Appa when you want something," she suspected, eyeing the elegantly decorated table.

"Oh, don't worry Amita. They'll get to that soon enough." Mr. Clements grinned, knowing exactly what this was all about. He often thought Wren had a heart like his mother's. She was incredibly intelligent and witty and wore her heart on her sleeve. And while Wren was not as warm to people, he could see it whenever she was with Rohit. Friendship was a beautiful thing, and Michael Clements was grateful to Rohit for making his daughter more human every day.

The families ate dinner and talked about their children's life after their hard work. Ria, Rohit's younger sister, sat at the table pushing her food around with her fork, annoyed that all her family could talk about for so many years was Rohit's success and college.

"Bet you're excited to be an only child in the fall." Wren nudged Ria in the shoulder.

"Trust me. I've been waiting my whole life for this," Ria muttered between bites. She was the second born, and that meant she was either destined to be exactly like her brother, or beat him. The sooner he left the house, the sooner she could try the latter.

"Ria, don't talk poorly about your brother," they heard Mr. Kumar say.

"Don't worry. We're just joking." Wren addressed him, and then she sent a wink Ria's way.

Ria's strained face cracked a smile. She couldn't wait for the fall to come, but that also meant she would have to say goodbye to Wren. She idolized Wren and often thought she was smarter than any teacher she had in school. Wren would miss Ria too, but not in the same way Ria would miss her. Losing Wren would be like losing a best friend or a big sister.

"Are we going to talk about what it is these kids want now?" Mrs. Kumar started.

"It better not be some stupid senior prank. I never understood those. These teachers spend a lifetime educating generations to come, and how do the students thank them? By filling the gym with water balloons or sticking forks all over the campus," Mr. Kumar chimed in.

"No, it's not a prank. We actually... why don't you tell them, Ro?" Wren glared at him.

"You got it, Wren." His voice quivered.

Wren pinched him hard in the arm. He yelped and then promptly cleared his throat, trying to mask his embarrassment.

"Wren and I were talking about growing up. We spent twelve years of our lives studying and researching, all to get to this point. And now we're here. Just seems like we should do something to celebrate."

"What? A grad party isn't enough praise?" Ria scoffed.

"No, it is. It's just... Wren and I want to sneak out for a night. Just one night. We won't leave town, but we'll be out all night and return just before morning."

The Kumars' eyes could have popped out of their sockets. Ria was on the verge of laughter. They couldn't tell if this was some sort of practical joke or if he was serious.

"Stupid. Right?" Wren's mother snorted.

"Vanessa, they're joking. Right?" Amita asked her desperately.

Mr. Kumar eyes moved from Rohit's face of disappointment to Wren's beckoning eyes, and out of some whirlwind of confusion and betrayal he spat out, "Log kya kahenge?"

What will people think?

Those three words pretty much defined a major consequence for any action. If Rohit wanted to go on a date, *log kya kahenge?* If he wanted to quit a sport, *log kya kahenge?* Wren knew this because it was unspoken in her family. It wasn't so much of a question as it was an order. She knew that people will look at you and wait for you to mess up. But she also knew that if people didn't change things up every once in a while, living life the same way would be a waste of life in general.

Rohit looked at Wren for some support. He caught that look in her eyes when she first came up with the idea for a night out. She wanted it, and therefore he wanted it too. On some level, maybe they even needed it. After all, he was growing tired of his parents' commands. He thought about rolling his eyes at the mere memory of that morning.

"What people, Dad? Who is watching me like a hawk? People don't need to know everything. I just need to live my life," Rohit spoke up.

"Live *your* life? And you think sneaking out with a girl doing god knows what is living?"

His parents were disgusted. Wren expected that. They knew Wren and Rohit would never date, but anytime they didn't want him to do something they acted like Wren and Rohit were secretly up to no good. Rohit had assured her that it was not to be taken personally and it was simply another Indian thing.

"Don't be like that..."

"If I may," Wren's father interrupted. "I know it's a lot. We sure as hell wouldn't have agreed to it if we thought they would do something dangerous. But look at them. They're good kids. They've worked together for so many years all to make sure they would get to where they are now. Let them have one night if that's all they want. Honestly, I think they'll probably end up at some twenty-four-hour library or something. We live in a good town, with good people, and these kids are responsible. I highly doubt anything dangerous will happen. They're so much smarter than that."

Wren knew from a young age that there were two types of lawyers. There were the ruthless ones looking for the blood in the water, like her mother, or there were ones that played off of emotions. Michael Clements was no doubt one of the best lawyers seen in the Philadelphia area, but he never made it a point to jam information in front of the judge and jury. His argument was very much a "how would you feel if…" mentality, and it worked for him.

The Kumars considered his argument. Rohit took out the contract and showed it to them. The contract was more than a piece of paper. It was better than an ask and answer. It was a mutual agreement between adults. It was their parents finally seeing them as equals, and after only a moment's hesitation, they agreed and signed.

If only they hadn't.

Chapter 7

——

The next afternoon, Wren dreamt she was swimming. She dove deep into a crystal blue ocean and was washed over with cool serenity. Light filled her every crease as the waves parted effortlessly to keep her moving.

Forward and forward.

Deeper and deeper.

Suddenly, the water filled her lungs like a ship about to capsize. Her arms turned to noodles as she flailed them around, searching for someone to help her. The waves darkened and swirled in riptides, crashing harder and harder. It swallowed her entirely, and she blinked, thinking for a spare minute she could see a world underneath the water. Just a flicker. Just a glimpse. She dove deeper as her lungs cried out for help. She wanted to go deeper and see what lies underneath, but her body stung with life and an itch to resurface. She stretched her arms above, reaching to get higher and higher as the air left entirely and worlds started to blur.

Wren woke up from her nap with a salty taste in her mouth that made her want to puke. Weakness crept through her vulnerable mind, making her feel like she was robbed and violated. It was like she was under the attack of her own brain. Like she was her greatest enemy.

Like most things that troubled her, she simply blinked it away as insignificant. Her brain was full and only had room to make space for more knowledge. She wasn't making room for the infection of self-doubt and failure anymore.

Her phone buzzed her to life. A text, from Asa. Her nerves tingled. What a high a boy could give her.

Asa: wanna meet up later? we can grab shakes :)

A date. Or practically one. Her heart rushed with blood and adrenaline and everything in between.

Wren: Meet you at Sundae's in an hour

Should she have added a smiley face or something more playful? She hesitated for a split second. She didn't want to be too forward.

Wren: :)

She did it anyway.

Sundae's was a famous ice cream shop in her town. It had been the hub for all of Richmond High to hang out at. You could almost always find people you knew there. Wren had been there a number of times, but with Ro, not a boy.

A *boy* boy.

She felt something turn in her stomach. It felt like she needed to hold herself back from trembling with excitement. This was the first time they were ever going to hang out together. Alone.

"Ro, I'm so scared. I can't even get this eyeliner to go on smoothly!" she yelled through facetime.

"Your hands are shaking," he noted.

"I know! I can't get them to stop! Ugh, the lines are gonna be uneven."

"They're fine. You look good, Wren."

"I wish I was better at this stuff."

"Wren! You will look fine no matter what. You don't have to try and impress him anymore. It'll be okay." Rohit promised with a warm look in his eyes. Her first date nerves made his insides burn. He knew he was going to have to let her go.

"Thanks, Ro."

Wren took off in an ivory blouse, an old pair of blue jeans, and her Converse. Her hair had been done up in two braids for the whole day and now fell past her shoulders in a tumble of thick waves.

She wanted to look good, professional. Not professional. This was not the same as a job interview. This was casually hanging out with a boy her own age. A boy who, for some odd reason, seemed to be showing interest in her. Wren wanted to deny that he could possibly like her back, but she was too good at reading men that she knew deep down it was true. He liked her.

That made her giddy.

Sundae's at this time of day was almost always empty. Wren often wondered why they didn't just stay open all night instead of closing at 2:00 a.m. No one came in the day, except for maybe the soccer moms getting a couple sundaes for whiny children in the evening. The high school students would start rolling in at about 8:00 p.m., and while Sundae's would close up, they would hang around the tables outside until 4:00, maybe even 5:00 in the morning.

Wren pulled into a parking spot next to Asa's white SUV. She could see him sitting at a picnic table outside. She felt every nerve in her body lift. She wanted to scream from excitement and puke at the same time. Her phone buzzed.

Rohit: Good luck. You got this.

Reassurance. Rohit always knew how she was feeling before she even realized it. He was good at that. He was the best friend she could ask for in that way.

With the push of her car door, Wren gathered all the courage she had and met Asa in a stride. He was wearing a heathered gray shirt and black shorts. *Ordinary.* He opened the shop door for her as she breathed him in. She couldn't get enough of it. She felt herself falling into a blissful coma over the next hour. She was floating on cloud nine, slowly coming back to life as her lips tingled each time Asa took a sip from his milkshake.

Asa felt the floor move beneath him every time she batted her eyelashes. His fingers drummed, excited, every time she laughed at his jokes.

"This is nice." Asa grinned, the tip of his foot against the tip of Wren's shoe.

"It is. How come we never did this sooner?"

"I don't know. We were both busy with school and everything else."

"It's a shame." Wren nodded.

"Huh?" Asa sat up, panic stricken.

"That we didn't hang out sooner. Not that *this* is a shame. This has been lovely." Wren assured him. It had been lovely. He was a gentleman. He put his phone away and even paid for her milkshake even though she heavily obliged.

Asa snorted. "Lovely. That's what you say when you invite neighbors over for dinner."

"No, that's not what I meant." Wren giggled. "I loved this," she found herself saying, inching forward.

Something passed between them. Maybe it was seconds or minutes, but the silence had been music to their ears. The air filled with nerves and not knowing what to say next. It was magic.

The bells on the door jingled as a large figure stepped forward, taking in the parlor. Asa put his hand up in a wave. Wren turned to find Mr. Alcott, their economics teacher, standing by the entrance eyeing his students, wondering if it was too late to leave and come back later to avoid an awkward interaction outside of the classroom.

"Mr. Alcott, how's your weekend going?" Asa called.

"Good, Mr. Mitchell. Thank you for asking. I hope you and Miss Clements are enjoying yourselves." This had made Wren whip her head back. She flashed him a smile, and he replied with a slight drop in his face. He went up to the counter and ordered a large banana split, two spoons, and disappeared into the parking lot.

"That was unusual," Wren found herself saying.

"I know. I would have thought he was more of a single scoop of pistachio kind of guy."

"No, not that. He was almost... pleasant."

"You sound shocked. Obviously, Mr. Alcott has a life outside of school."

Wren thought about this. It surely didn't seem like it. She caught herself before her mind spiraled into different thoughts. She was ruining her time with Asa. She wanted to stay there forever.

"We should do this again sometime." Asa smiled, playing with his straw.

"We are. You know, with the whole sneaking out thing?"

"I know, but I mean even after that. Just the two of us... if that's okay with you?"

Wren felt all the heat in the world rush to her cheeks. She didn't know feelings made her weak, but at this point, she was willing to wave a white flag.

"Are you asking me out on another date?"

"So this is a date then?" Asa grinned.

She'd seen playful banter like this in movies. "I think you already know that."

He kissed her on the cheek before they got in their cars and went separate ways. She wished she could replay that moment over and over again. It was the perfect time to brush his lips against hers, but he hadn't, leaving something big to look forward to.

Chapter 8

The date was such a dream that Wren had almost forgot about the plan to sneak out.

"We're gonna die. We're gonna die. We're gonna die," Rohit chanted the next day at school as if somehow it would convince Wren that they could just call off the plan. She wasn't going to do anything of the sort. Her heart fluttered with excitement merely thinking about how she would be able to casually hang out with Asa again.

That night would change everything for her and Rohit. After all, this was the make-or-break moment of their lives. Their group chat buzzed to life seemingly overnight. For once, the pair felt like they had a group. It felt like they had places to be and people to see, and that night they surely did. It was almost impossible to make it through school that day. It had been excruciatingly long and dull.

"Ro, you're, like, falling apart. Lighten up," Wren advised, noticing Rohit biting his nails raw.

"Yeah, Ro. Lighten up." Derek smirked. Derek Sanders had decided to meet them by their lockers before lunch to chat. They became fast friends, and especially with someone they hardly knew for the past four years. Who knew that a simple invitation could change the outcome of friendship?

It was then that Wren realized she was capable of much more. She was capable of being normal. She was able to make friends without overcorrecting them, and she turned out to be much better at socializing than she thought. Maybe if her mother hadn't expected her to be perfect all the time, she could be that Wren. *Normal* Wren.

"How are you so cool about this?" Rohit muttered, taking his books out of his locker with a sweaty hand.

"I'm the one who came up with this idea in the first place, if you remember."

"Genius, if you ask me. You guys really didn't think you were going to go to college without experiencing this stuff, did you?" Derek complimented, biting into an apple from his lunch.

"What's wrong with that?" Rohit fired back.

"That's suicide, bro. That's how you end up on the floor of a frat, or so baked that they need to call medical on you. Think of it as training. Or... studying. You experience it all and learn your limits before you go out into the real world and do it."

"See? It's smart. Logical, even. Lighten up, Ro. What's the worst that could happen?"

"We could get arrested for underaged drinking, possession of illegal drugs, trespassing, and vandalism."

Wren spoke in a British accent. "Or worse: *expelled*."

Derek chuckled at the *Harry Potter* joke, waived a quick goodbye, and headed for lunch.

"Ro, calm down. We're doing this because we've missed out on being rebellious our whole lives. One day isn't going to change everything," Wren reassured him.

"But what if it does?"

"Then isn't it better living life the way you want to? If you don't know what it's like, how do you know if the life you have is the life for you?"

His face softened and took her in. She was wearing a white dress that fell just in the middle of her thighs and was lined with a flower trim. Wren, no matter how much studying she did, always made it a point to look nice for school. She didn't care that most people went to school in clothes they went to sleep in. She liked looking nice because she simply wanted to. He wished he could do things simply because he wanted to. He wished he could come to school in a hoodie and basketball shorts all the time, but his parents would say he wasn't dressed appropriately and make him change into his usual smart casual attire. His parents never grew out of the professional attire from their Indian schools growing up. If Rohit didn't attempt to dress well, they would see him as any other kid. And he was not just any other kid.

Wren followed Derek off to lunch and to talk to Valerie about something, leaving Rohit alone with his thoughts. Just then, his eyes found Stella Lu opening her locker only to have a dozen things fall out in a landslide. While everyone else had decided to steer clear of Stella and her unpleasant attitude, Rohit made his way over to her.

He knelt down and helped collect her things before they were trampled on by those who passed by in the hallway.

"You don't have to." She flushed, a bit self-conscious.

"It's no trouble. You should really clean that locker though." Rohit mustered a smile.

"Hmm. Yeah, with all the time I have on my hands," she replied with a twinge of sarcasm.

He looked down at the mess. Most of them were ripped up pieces of paper and old tests.

"We could just toss this stuff out. Looks like old scraps."

"No!" Stella fired back.

Rohit put his hands up in surrender. He nodded and moved his books off to the side and continued to help Stella with her papers. "I didn't know you were such a hoarder, Stella." He chuckled.

"Just sentimental."

Rohit furrowed an eyebrow. "I thought you never had time to be sentimental. You know, with all the Ivy League prep and whatnot."

Stella had been so close to being the same as Wren and Rohit, but she lacked something. That very same factor was what Stella saw as a weakness.

"Yeah. Well, things change when you can't afford an Ivy and you have to go to University of Michigan." She wanted to ignore the fact that maybe it was her own damn fault that she was going to Michigan instead of to an Ivy. Stella knew how to sell it though. She would say that she got into MIT, Cornell, Dartmouth, and Stanford, but she chose University of Michigan because it was the most affordable option and she liked the program more.

She would make it seem like it was the smart option, not that she had gotten waitlisted at all of those schools. They were schools she would have accepted in a heartbeat if it meant that she could fulfill her life-long dream of attending an Ivy league school. But she wasn't accepted, and that hurt the most. Perhaps she should have applied to more backup schools, and perhaps she shouldn't have oversold her capabilities. Perhaps she should have lived a little anyway if this is where she would end up.

Perhaps perfection wasn't enough.

Chapter 9

———

School had dragged on long enough.

Wren was bursting with excitement until she realized she had absolutely nothing to wear that night. Her closet consisted of what she liked to call "comfort cute." She wore tons of sweaters and straight leg jeans. She even wore skirts and dresses when she felt like getting more dressed up, but nothing in comparison to what she would need that night. The closest thing to a crop top that she could find was an old tank top from sixth grade pre-puberty. And that's how she found herself at Valerie's house that evening.

"Sorry about the mess," Valerie apologized, switching on twinkly lights, illuminating the walls of her room. She dropped her bag on her Persian rug and flopped into a cluster of sage green and yellow throw pillows on her bed.

"Mess?" Wren laughed, passing through her room. It looked like it was straight out of a Pinterest board.

"I don't know... sometimes the plants and flowers can be a lot for people." Valerie pointed to the fake green vines hanging from her wall and artificial flowers crawling up her door. Beside the door were taped pictures of Big Ben, record players, museums, and beautiful European buildings. It all looked so chic to Wren, like it was a part of some fabulous dreamy old movie. They made Wren feel warm inside, as if looking at them long enough could take her there.

"A lot prettier than PA, right?" Valerie suggested from behind Wren.

"I didn't know you were so into Europe," Wren confessed.

"Yeah. Well, you gotta learn a lot about a place that you're going to live in a couple of months."

Wren's chest contracted inside of her as heat flushed through her face. Wren had never actually shown any interest in knowing anyone's future except for hers and Rohit's.

"You're moving to Europe?" Wren stammered.

"Yeah. I'm going to the University College of London in the fall. But I hope I get to live in some other cities after my undergrad."

"Valerie, I... I'm so sorry, I never knew you were going to London. That's amazing. Congratulations!"

Valerie blushed, but something new flickered in her eyes that she tried to blink away.

"What's wrong?"

"Nothing."

Wren raised her eyebrows, not buying the lie. Defeated, Valerie knew Wren long enough to know she always had to have the answer, and she would have to confess her true feelings to Wren.

"It's just... this is something I've wanted my whole life. What if I don't like it there, or if I find out I'm not good at architecture?"

Another pang of guilt hit Wren. She hadn't even realized Valerie was interested in architecture even though all the signs were there. She was always visiting Philadelphia and posting pictures by city hall. She had pictures of historical European buildings up on her walls like it was inspiration. "That's kind of the leap of faith we all take when we leave home," Wren found herself saying. "The fear of the unknown, the fear of not being good enough, the fear of having to come back. Go there and become a badass architect. Visit all sorts of cities and stare in awe at those buildings. Even if your feelings change, at least you'll be surrounded by something you love. At least you'll be living the life you want," Wren explained, hoping to make up for her lack of knowing.

Somehow, Wren had taken that fear and eased it. Valerie was grateful for that. "Thanks, babe." She smiled. "Anyway, you came here to borrow something for tonight."

She quickly got up and opened her closet doors. They were filled with color-coded racks in a mesmerizing gradient of whites and yellows to purples and blacks. Her closet emulated fancy racks of one-of-a-kinds that belonged in expensive boutiques.

"You have a shit ton of clothes." Wren observed as Valerie began pulling out crop tops, mini-skirts, and denim jackets.

"Don't hate me, but I think most Americans dress like trash bags. The appeal of wearing a hoodie and sweats every day is still a mystery to me. I wish I didn't have to constantly dress down my own style just to not stick out like a sore thumb," Valerie dished while sifting through more European pieces. Her fingers traced berets and chic leather dresses in longing. Wren could practically see Valerie sipping coffee in a café, all done up in a trendy outfit and fitting perfectly into place.

"Valerie, I don't think anyone would say you *stuck out*. I think if you just wear what you want, you'd find a lot of people in school trying to dress more like you."

"Easier said than done." She shrugged. "So what do you wanna wear? A dress, a skirt?"

"I don't know. Maybe something comfortable and only a little bold for me?"

"How about a sexy crop top and jeans? Still super comfortable, very flattering, and people won't be able to keep their eyes off of you."

"Let's see them."

***

Tyler Harrison skated up to his house that evening and found himself questioning exactly what he was getting into. He could still call the whole thing off. Two newbies and a ton of weed did not sound like something he wanted to be a part of, but it ended up being something he couldn't say no to.

His pocket vibrated. Tyler's eyes rolled as he let out a groan. "Fucking group chats," he muttered as he opened the text.

Mia: getting the alc together soon. so just some claws, hard lemonades, and 2 fifths of svedka?

Her text message was followed by three thumbs up, the verdict filtering in. Tyler let out another groan. Whatever happened to an old-fashioned beer?

He tossed his phone back into his shorts pocket and wiped his face with the hem of his shirt. He wrapped his sweaty fingers around the handles of the trash cans and began to wheel them back up his driveway until a rattle sounded from the house over. Sammy Rodriguez was doing the same thing.

Something tight grew in his stomach. Why did it always have to be like this? There was this silence between them all the time. Why did they have to just be acquaintances? Wouldn't it be best to just put all that aside and be more friendly? He wrestled with the thought, and just before Sammy disappeared behind the bushes Tyler found himself skating her way.

"Sammy."

She whipped her curly head around, completely surprised to see Tyler Harrison behind her, calling her name. "Hey, Tyler. What's up?" Something raised in her voice.

"Hey... I just wanted to say 'hey.'"

"Hey." Sammy turned her back on him and started walking to her house again.

"How come we don't talk?" Tyler shouted from behind her.

"We do talk, Tyler."

"No. We walk home together when parties die down. The extent of our conversations are drunk and high afterthoughts."

"So what?"

"We've been neighbors since eighth grade. Don't you think it's odd that we haven't had a real conversation?"

"I don't know. It's not *that* weird," she muttered, a note of defensiveness cracking.

Tyler didn't miss it. "Relax, Sammy. I just wanted to have a casual conversation. We don't have to be best friends or anything."

"Well, we can talk tonight. You know, at the thing?"

"Yeah. Sure, Sammy." Tyler shrugged, digging his hands deep in his pockets and turning around on his heel.

Sammy didn't know what compelled her to do it, but maybe part of her wanted to rewrite her story. Sammy, the friend, instead of Sammy, that girl who always goes a little too hard at parties.

"Wait. Do you want to come inside?"

Tyler turned back to face her, his body perking up slightly. "You don't have to..."

"Tyler, just get in here." Sammy laughed, wheeling the trash can off to the side of her garage.

Tyler left his skateboard outside and followed Sammy inside her house, the aroma of Latin spices hitting his nose. He followed her down the stairs into her basement where she plopped herself on an old couch and popped open the mini fridge. She tossed him a ginger ale and pulled out a bottle of water for herself. "You can sit down, Tyler."

He sat on the other end of the couch and cracked open his soda. "You remembered." He smiled.

"We see each other every weekend. It would be ridiculous if I didn't notice how you mix ginger ale with every drink and crave it when you're high." Sammy smirked. "So… what did you want to talk about?"

Tyler took a gulp, letting the carbonation dance over his tongue. He thought for a moment. He never actually knew too much about Sammy, just that he always walked her home after parties. He brought up the only thing that seemed relevant, "Isn't it kinda odd that we're, like, teaching Wren and Rohit how to party? They're like geniuses, can't they figure it out themselves? It's not rocket science."

"Maybe not to you, but it must be hard for them. To not already be thrown into that environment and then suddenly want it…" Sammy thought about what she would be doing if she wasn't in that environment every weekend. Instead of hooking up with classmates and drinking too much, would she be bettering herself, or tearing herself down in another way?

"That's true. I'm just nervous. If something goes wrong at the party or if one of them gets way too drunk…"

"We'll know what to do. That's the whole point of us going. At least for me… I'll be on mom duty and make sure the kids are alright." She smiled, jokingly.

"Oh, Sammy. You're never in mom mode." Tyler took another sip of his soda.

"Yeah…" Memories of downing cups of jungle juice and checking her weight in the mirror every hour resurfaced. "Well, tonight is a night for changes."

***

Mia sighed as she pulled up to the liquor store at the end of an empty strip mall. She turned up her car radio, waiting for the text telling her she could go inside, see her boyfriend Leo, and collect the bottles.

She hated this part. She felt like a baby, latching onto the nearest adult so they could handle grown up things for her. It was just about the only tension in their relationship, but after high school was over she wouldn't need to ask for favors anymore. She could move in with her boyfriend and leave all the underaged high school antics behind her. She could give up cheap booze at parties with sticky floors for dry bottles of wine and evenings alone with Leo, who would eventually graduate from night classes and studying.

Mia watched as a customer left the store, case in hands, and dumped it into his car. As soon as he sped off, she waited a minute before driving her car behind the store where the security cameras were just for show and never actually worked. In fact, for a liquor store, the owner really didn't care about making sure the security system functioned at all. Only the camera out front was live to monitor who was coming in and out of the store, but they never managed to check the back. Mia jumped at the sound of the back door pushing open, her buff boyfriend with arms the size of her thighs twitching with excitement to see her.

"Hey, Mia mush." Leo grinned like a child, sticking his head through her open window and planting a soft kiss on her cheek.

She rolled her eyes, though she loved it and he knew it. "Hey, baby." She took him in, seeing the droopiness of his eyes, studying all day no doubt. She pulled him by the neck, kissing him properly and passionately, biting his lip a bit. She gave Leo a look... *the* look.

Instant energy filled his face and veins. Mia smirked at how easy it was to turn his day around. She had been happy to do it anyway. After all, with his daytime shifts and night classes, she barely got laid anymore. Just the feeling of his arms made her body ache for him to be all over her.

"Really? Right now?" He looked around him, concerned. "What if a customer goes inside? I won't know they're there."

Mia bit her lip, feeling all sorts of sexual tension in the air. She unbuckled her seatbelt and stuck her head through the window to whisper in his ear. "Let's go inside then. Back office? I think it's about time for your break." And then she nibbled his ear.

That was all it took. His fingers flung her car door open, and she jumped into his arms, wrapping her legs around his waist. He kissed her all the way to the break room, careful to check every few seconds to make sure no one came through the door. She brushed against his soft lips, then cheek, making her way to his ear. She nibbled it, feeling the way his body yearned for more. He pushed her head aside and bit her neck the way he knew she liked it. His fingers were in her denim skirt when they heard a noise from the door.

"Oh fuck." Derek stopped for a second before turning around and shielding his eyes behind a paint speckled hand. "Mia, what the fuck?"

"Derek!" She gasped, pushing her boyfriend off of her and quickly readjusting her hair and clothes. "Sorry," she whispered to her boyfriend, giving him a quick peck. "We'll continue this later."

"What are you doing here, Sanders?" Mia's boyfriend sighed, running his fingers through his hair. He was trying to not look pissed off that Derek had just interrupted his alone time with his girlfriend.

Derek peeked through the hand he was hiding behind to make sure the pair was decent and eventually put it down and at his side with a sigh. "Mia told me to meet her here. She wanted me to bring half the stuff to the thing tonight."

"Oh... so you're here for alcohol." Leo sighed, shooting a disappointed look at Mia. His stomach twisted a knot inside.

Mia looked from Leo to Derek, clearly sensing her boyfriend's tension. "Derek, you have to go. The security camera would have caught you when you came through the front doors, so meet us around back instead."

With that, Derek walked away from them, throwing the hood of his sweatshirt over his paint speckled hair before exiting through the front doors.

"Again, Mia?" Leo sighed, disappointed.

"I didn't come here just for that. C'mon. Don't be mad at me." Mia pouted, placing her hand on his chest, knowing that her boyfriend couldn't stay mad at her when she looked at him like that.

He groaned. "What do you need?"

Mia smiled and threw her arms around him. She tasted his lips again, taking in the flavor of energy drinks and minty gum. "Thank you." She kissed him again. "Thank you," and again, "and thank you." Mia only let her tough exterior down when she was with her boyfriend. He could make her melt, and everyone else merely irritated her unless she had a drink in hand.

They heard a knock at the back door and let Derek inside. Leo clapped him on the back and apologized for walking in on him and Mia. They laughed like Leo was back in high school again, and each split up to round up the supplies for the night. Leo helped them load cases into Derek and Mia's cars, each of them taking a bottle with them as well. Leo waved a goodbye to them before beating it to the register as soon as a customer came through the front doors.

Derek clinked his bottle against Mia's as if they were close friends. "Sorry about before."

"Not your fault. I forgot you were meeting me, and it was dumb. Sorry you had to see us... you know..."

"Oh, no. That's not what I meant. I mean, I am sorry for that, but it seemed like there was some tension when I said I was there to pick up the stuff. I didn't mean to cause any problems between you guys," Derek apologized, wholeheartedly.

Mia looked at him with calculating eyes. She didn't really know Derek Sanders, and frankly, she didn't plan on getting to know him. She didn't need him to get to know her either.

"It's whatever." She shrugged. "See you tonight." And with that, she dropped the bottle in the passenger's seat and closed her door. She put the keys in the ignition, ready to drive away, but she popped her head through the window again. "Stick to painting, artsy boy. If you try to have a *real* conversation with me tonight, I'm going to get you so fucking drunk that you won't be able to hold a paintbrush straight for the rest of your life."

He smirked. "Looking forward to it, Mia."

Chapter 10

Wren's heart was beating out of her chest. Her hands were slick with sweat and couldn't stop trembling. She found herself at the mirror for the fifth time that night.

"This is going to be great," she told herself, clenching her sides, readjusting the unfamiliar polyester wrapped around her torso. Softer tones were normally her best friend, but for some reason she was drawn to Valerie's crimson red crop top. She watched how the fabric seemed to simply stretch across her curves and hug her soft skin. She hardly recognized herself, clothed in this new persona, owning the difference in the way she held herself, every dip in the blouse, the way it drew eyes to a specific place. It was daring.

All of a sudden, buzzing sounded from her back pocket, snapping her back into reality.

Mia: there in 5.

Sammy: me and Tyler are almost there

Derek: OMW

Valerie: be there soon

Asa: see you guys in a few

Wren descended the stairs with a tiptoe, and when her fingers wrapped around the door handle and pulled, the night air filled her lungs with relief. She inhaled deeply, drinking in the anticipation of the night, taking note of what an escape from reality felt like. A shadow met her eyes at the end of her driveway. The outline of its broad shoulders and long arms were all too familiar to Wren. She made her way past the shadows of her house to meet a nervous Rohit at the end of the driveway.

"Last chance to back out, Wren. I think they'll all be fine without us." He shrugged, ready to turn his heel at her say so.

"I'm not chickening out, Ro! I'm ready!" She exclaimed, intoxicated with excitement.

"Ready for what?" He asked, not expecting an answer.

"To live a little."

Houses and streetlights passed them in minutes while they walked over to the park. Trees closed around them as they found their gang at the meeting point, circled around a few bags filled to the brim.

"They're here!" Valerie pointed out, making her way over to hug both Wren and Rohit.

"Hey, Valerie..." He coughed awkwardly. "...everyone." Rohit nodded to the group in front of him.

Valerie pulled Wren and Rohit by their wrists toward the inner circle in excitement.

Wren stole a glance at Asa, feeling her face flush. *Be cool*, she told herself. She didn't want this adventure to just be about him. Even though she couldn't stop thinking

There are two sides to everyone...

about their date and the potential of another one, she wanted this outing to be special for a number of reasons.

Despite her promise to not get too infatuated so early in the night, Asa inched closer to Wren all of a sudden, like it was familiar and routine. Goosebumps crawled up Wren's arms with each step he made to her. He was particularly awestricken. His eyes flicked from her golden hair clip that pulled her hair to the side to the dainty gold necklace that hung around her neck. He took note of how she was glowing in red instead of her normal muted and soft tones. Rohit had noticed that too and clenched his fist as he saw Asa nearly closing the space between him and Wren.

"You look great." Asa breathed, taking her in.

"Thanks. You too." She grinned, eyeing his blue shirt and jeans. *The way he looked good in everything,* she thought.

"Alright, enough chit chat," Derek started. "Let's get started!"

"Okay. So, I was thinking that first we could get a little tipsy, then go to the party Sammy's taking us to, then we could do a couple of Valerie's famous dares, paint the streets courtesy of Derek, and end the night on a literal high, thanks to Tyler," Wren finished, with a look of accomplishment plastered on her face.

"Damn, Wren. I was just thinking about seeing what the vibes were and go from there." Tyler blinked.

"Nerd," Mia coughed to herself.

"I think it sounds like a good idea," Sammy backed Wren up. "If they want to do everything, then we need to make time to do it all."

Tyler dug his hand in a bag and pulled out a bottle triumphantly. "Then let's get fucking drunk," he said with a wide toothed grin.

Everyone started pulling cans and bottles out of the bag like it was candy. Wren found herself holding a mango flavored White Claw and clinking it against everyone else's drinks in celebration. The crisp bubbles filled her mouth with refreshing fruit. She was relieved. It didn't taste that strong at all. She was terrified she would despise the taste of alcohol and the whole night would be a bust, but this was turning out to be quite the opposite. Before she knew it her drink was done, and Mia had pulled out a multicolored bottle. She slid the cap off and pulled out disposable shot glasses, filling them to the brim with clear liquid.

"What is it?" Rohit asked when she handed him the shot.

"Pink lemonade." She winked.

Rohit raised his eyebrows, unfooled.

"It's pink lemonade *flavored*. It's vodka, my dude. If you wanna get drunk, this will get you there," Mia explained while handing the rest of the shots out, ending on Wren.

Wren stared at the clear liquid. It smelled bitter and like something she would use to clean a wound. Suddenly, a knot in her stomach grew.

"I don't know if I want it," Wren found herself saying.

"You're the one who wanted to get drunk. Right?" Mia challenged, a tone of irritation spiking in her voice.

"Yeah, but..."

"If she doesn't want to drink it, she doesn't have to," Rohit interjected, protective over his best friend. Something in Wren kicked at her insides. This *is* what she wanted.

"Yeah, no peer pressure!" Derek hollered with a chuckle before taking his shot in a single gulp without even flinching.

"No one's going to force you, Wren. It's your choice," Sammy reassured her.

This is what I wanted. And just like that, Wren closed her eyes, brought the cup to her lips, and downed it as fast as she could. It burned the whole way down. The bitter taste lingered on her tongue, and her throat flared up in defiance. Then her insides fired with heat. She opened her eyes and started to cough.

Everyone around her cheered triumphantly at Wren's first major milestone. Almost everyone. Amidst the celebratory hoots, Rohit's face contorted. This was happening, whether he wanted it to or not.

Another drink later and the gang decided to follow Sammy to the party that Grant Davenport, the popular boy, was throwing. They found themselves passing by houses that seemingly kept getting larger. Music blared from the distance as groups of friends raced each other to the house. Wren's head was buzzing with excitement. Suddenly, everything felt easier. Any weight that had been on her shoulders had been lifted, and she absorbed the mentality that all she needed to worry about was the now. What a beautiful high life was.

A huge shadow cast over them and a gorgeous mansion appeared before their eyes. The lawn was littered with red cups and the windows were lit up with neon lights. Music seemed to pound through every bone in their bodies. Wren and Rohit absentmindedly followed everyone in, the unfamiliar scene suddenly becoming the place they needed to be.

As soon as they stepped foot inside, a slick stickiness in the air made everything warm and fuzzy. Bodies were crashing into other bodies as screams and laughter called from every direction. Hands were wet with beer or sweat, to which Wren and Rohit found themselves not wanting to know which one. Suddenly, Sammy was throwing her arms around the back of a boy's neck, embracing him in a deep hug. Grant Davenport turned around with a movie star smile and hugged her back.

"Sammy! I was wondering how long it would take for you to get here." He nudged, spilling a little bit of beer.

"Well, these days I'm traveling with a crew." She grinned, nodding in the direction of everyone else.

"Tyler, my man!" He thrust his hand toward Tyler in a familiar handshake. "Derek, Val, always a pleasure. Oh damn, you got Mitchell here? Dude, I almost never see you here anymore." He threw his arm around Asa as if they were pals. Then his eyes lifted, and for a split second he thought his mind was playing tricks on him. "Woah. Isn't there, like, some extra credit you guys need to get started on?" Grant laughed, addressing Wren and Rohit.

Wren laughed with Grant. Rohit, however, felt his fist clench.

"Be nice, Grant. There's a first time for everyone," Sammy pointed out, shoving him in the shoulder.

"Of course." Grant turned back to Wren and held her hand sympathetically. "I apologize. That's no way for a host to treat his guests." He apologized sincerely, giving her hand a squeeze.

Rohit shifted uncontrollably and lifted his hand to pull Wren's arm away from Grant's clutch. She shrugged Rohit off and shot him a glare.

"Drinks are in the kitchen. No one's driving. Right?" He looked around the circle.

Wren put her free hand on top of his. "Swear." She smiled.

"Great." His movie star grin never dipped. "You guys are in great hands. Sammy is here all the time. She knows where everything is." As quick as he appeared in their sight, he disappeared back into the sea of drunken teens on the dance floor.

Sammy grabbed Valerie's wrist, who grabbed Asa's, who then continued the chain as Sammy pulled them toward the kitchen. A keg sat by the countertop surrounded by a sea of red cups. Wren's hand knocked down a few empty liquor bottles as she went to get herself a beer.

"Why don't you wait a little before the next drink babe." Valerie told her, her hand over the cup Wren was just about to grab. "It's your first time, and I think you should pace yourself so you don't end up on the floor." She winked.

Wren nodded her head, and instead Valerie led her, Rohit, and Asa past a couple attached at the lips into the backyard. There must have been a fifteen-degree difference in the temperature inside compared to outside.

"Much cooler out here, right? God, I can never stay inside for that long." Valerie exhaled, fanning her face and tugging at the neckline of her dress.

Rohit's fingertips grazed the top of a table lined with cups in a triangle.

"You play?" Asa asked him, nearing the table.

"No. I, uhh... just curious," Rohit stammered, nervous for what he might get himself into.

"Well, c'mon. Let's play. It's super easy to learn. We'll do teams." Asa grinned, fixing the cups.

Rohit's eyes darted from the cups to Wren. His fingers closed around a ping pong ball, and he spun it on the slick table top. "Okay. Me and Wren versus you and Val?" Rohit gestured for Wren to join on his side.

"Actually, Rohit, I was thinking you and I could be a team," Valerie interjected. She made her way to his side of the table, picked the ball up, and dipped it in a cup.

"Okay. Wren, you're on mine then." Asa slid to make room for her.

Valerie caught a glimpse of the droop in Rohit's eyes. She nudged him with her shoulder. "It's even this way. You guys haven't played before. Now you've got some experience on your side."

He nodded as Asa began to explain the rules. No elbows past the table, a bounce into a cup got two out, and more rules like that. Then, it was time to see who went first. Asa and Valerie demonstrated, covering their eyes with a hand, counting off 'til three, and seeing who sunk a ball into a cup. A plop sounded, and Valerie's ball landed in a cup to Wren's right. They were going first.

"Damn. She's got some skill," Asa pointed out, bouncing his ball across the table to Rohit.

"Hope I didn't make a mistake being on your team." Wren smiled, her fingers slowly inching toward his.

Plop.

Rohit sunk a ball right in front of them. "Less talking, more playing," Rohit announced, satisfied.

Valerie missed her shot. Asa went next, narrowly missing the back right cup. "Not too high, not too low. Don't worry, just have fun with it," Asa instructed Wren.

But she was nothing if not a perfectionist.

Chapter 11

"How are you so good at this?" Asa asked, in awe of how Wren hadn't missed a single cup since they started the game.

"Maybe it's just beginner's luck?" Wren offered with a smile.

"You're too good for beginner's luck. C'mon, seriously." Asa prodded with wonder in his eyes.

"Physics," she confessed with a grin.

"Wren, I gotta pee, babe. Come with?" Valerie half asked, grabbing Wren by the arm and pulling her inside.

She pulled Wren through entangled bodies all the way up the stairs into a massive bathroom. She let out a sigh of relief once they closed the door and immediately took out a tube of lipstick to reapply on her perfect lips.

"So, you and Asa? I gotta admit, I should have seen that coming," she said, readjusting her hair in the mirror.

"Is it obvious?" Wren's voice quivered with a twinge of anxiety.

"That you guys are all over each other? Listen, babe: you could be blind and still be able to see it."

"So you think he likes me back...?" For some reason, Wren felt her stomach turn. Goosebumps fired up every inch of her skin. She didn't know why she was suddenly feeling insecure.

"Why do you sound scared?" Valerie turned, tucking Wren's hair behind her ear.

Wren looked down at her shoes. "This doesn't normally happen. Maybe for you it happens, like, every day. And you get the option to turn people down. Guys like him... I don't know... He's way out of my league." Suddenly all her doubts she never realized had started pouring out. She read Asa well, but it was his feelings that were sometimes so hard to rationalize.

"Oh, Wren. I've got something to tell you. You are beautiful, sexy, and so goddamn smart. Babe *he's* the one who is lucky that you're into him."

Valerie gave Wren's hand a squeeze. Wren nodded, feeling too aware of her vulnerability again. Valerie noticed the uncomfortable shift, but was always prepared to help others. "I think I'm losing my buzz. We need a refresher. Don't tell the others I have this contraband." Valerie pulled up the side of her dress and unstrapped a flask from her leg.

"What is it?"

"Liquid courage." She took a swig and handed it to Wren. "Bottoms up, babe."

It burned all the way down. It hit her twice as hard as the vodka had. She was washed over with warmth and suddenly moving felt like she was swimming. Everything was easier.

"Good?" Valerie asked.

"They seriously have to make this stuff taste better." Wren laughed.

"Babe, tequila doesn't have to change for anyone."

Wren took another swig after Valerie. It went down much easier. She could get used to this—the way that only one thought popped into her mind at a time and how she could simply decide not to spiral. She enjoyed the simplicity in alcohol. Drink and feel things. A smile grew on her face. She felt the speakers pulsate through the floor.

"Val, I wanna dance."

"You got it, babe."

They raced to the stairs, following the vibrations. The rhythm intensified, matching up with every beat in Wren's heart. Her legs were warm and moved almost like she was floating down the stairs. She followed Valerie into the crowd, and another wave of warmth washed over her. Smiles and laughter surrounded her. People were singing along and moving effortlessly without a care in the world. She felt blissfully happy.

Oh, to not care about a damn thing. The thought made her do a twirl. A hand wrapped around hers. It was Rohit. Her smile widened. She kissed him on his cheek.

"Ro, I'm so happy we did this!" Wren shouted above the music.

"I'm happy you're happy," he replied with a tight smile. She looked magnificent, like something people would write stories about and tell their children. A princess in a far-off land, married a prince, slayed the dragon, lived happily ever after, the end. But she wasn't that simple. She was electric, to say the least.

A dark hand wrapped around Wren's waist and pulled her close. Rohit felt his face flush and left to get another drink. A smile stretched across Asa's face as he moved with Wren. She was surprisingly free. It was like he discovered something wonderful by accident. He smelled the liquor on her breath, but he didn't mind. He figured they would get to this part with or without the alcohol. He always intended to get close with her.

"You're beautiful, Wren." He spun her around, electricity in the air.

"Shut up." She smiled, enjoying his touch.

He moved his left hand around her waist, sending chills up her spine and traced his right fingers along her blushing cheek. He was inching closer, the scent of woodsy cologne and Old Spice sending her emotions over the edge. He closed his eyes, closing the space between them slowly.

"W-wait," Wren stammered, pulling away.

Asa was taken aback. His hands dropped. Wren saw the disappointment fill his eyes. She placed a hand on his chest, wanting to drown in the blues of his shirt. "Not yet. Not here," she explained. She wanted him more than she would have liked to admit. She wanted to feel his skin on hers. She wanted to taste his supple lips. She wanted it to be so special that no one else could ruin it.

"Okay." He nodded, re-lacing his fingers in hers, dancing through the next few songs by her side.

Their pockets vibrated in unison. It was the group chat.

Mia: Meet me in the basement. I think it's time for Valerie's dares.

Suddenly, the whole gang flocked to the basement doors to meet Mia and Derek by the bar. They were taking shots alone and laughing hysterically.

"Oh good, you're all here!" Derek exclaimed, gesturing all of them to take a seat on the couch.

"Val, we're in need of some dares. Derek and I are *verrry* drunk and need some entertainment ASAP. Gather round, kiddos. Y'all are gonna want some more alc in you before Val makes us do crazy shit." Mia dumped more liquor into everyone's cups. She had let down her tough exterior for the group.

I guess alcohol reveals the real you, thought Wren.

They all drank the contents of their cups and braced themselves for what was about to take place.

"We'll start easy," Valerie began.

"Oooh, that's what she always says before shit happens." Sammy giggled.

"We'll do truth or dare instead, since we've got some newbies. Sammy, truth or dare?"

"Dare, baby!" Sammy hollered.

"Makeout with Derek," Valerie commanded plainly, without batting an eye.

"You could have given me something harder," Sammy protested.

"C'mon. You don't wanna kiss me?" Derek pouted sarcastically.

"Just sit still and shut up," Sammy snapped back, making her way over and planting one on him.

Wren and Rohit's eyes grew wide as they realized how normal this was for everyone. Something as intimate as a kiss was something completely ordinary. It was like they were watching a movie, like some form of adrenaline filled the room, giving everyone a jolt. They went in a circle, answering questions or doing something outrageous, like Mia who was dared to go up to an occupied room and be the biggest, in Derek's words, "cock block" in the world.

Wren felt her heart beat out of her chest. She was overwhelmed with all that she had experienced so far, and it felt like she had just found Willy Wonka's golden ticket, or like she was Harry finding out he was a wizard. She had felt something wonderful, and she never wanted to let that go.

"Rohit. Your turn. Truth or dare?" Tyler grinned.

Rohit shifted uncomfortably in his seat. "Uhh, truth." He shrugged, thinking he was an open book.

"Who's the prettiest girl at this party?"

Rohit looked around as if he was suffocating in the room. He knew what the answer was. She was the prettiest girl all the time. She made him smile and laugh and feel just about everything in between. The suspense was killing him. Everyone stared at him, waiting to hear if their suspicions were confirmed or if he had harbored a bigger secret.

"Valerie," he choked out.

Wren let out a hoot, and he could have just died right there. Valerie tucked her hair behind her ear and tried to hide her flushed cheeks.

"I'll be back. I need some air." Rohit muttered, lifting himself off of the couch and racing for the door.

"Wren's turn," Valerie continued, moving on.

"Dare." Wren was sure of herself. It was different from the version of herself that was sure of answers on tests. It was a figment of an adrenaline junkie alter ego, but it powered her very soul in that moment.

Valerie thought about a dare for an electrifying minute or two, and all of a sudden she sat up with a smile. "You like to run, right?"

"Yeah."

"Good. I dare you to run through town, and we will text you where to go. Collect little keepsakes at each stop and bring them to us to prove you were there."

"That's a little weird and obscure," Wren replied, pulling her hair into a ponytail.

"Gotta mix things up, babe. Sometimes you gotta do stupid shit." Valerie waved a "goodbye" to her, and suddenly Wren was exiting the front doors at a jog, waiting for the first text.

The night air felt like a different world. Cold air crept up her spine as she darted into the night. She headed straight out of the neighborhood to the main road. A twig snapped from behind her, but when she looked back, it was just a squirrel scurrying back into the shadows.

Valerie: Florence Bookstore

Wren turned on her heel and headed left. She picked up her speed as darkness surrounded her, not a headlight to be seen for the next hundred yards. Her skin felt like it was swimming in the night. Her body was used to running early in the morning, but this was different. It was smooth like jazz music; it was swimming in a pool on a hot day. She didn't feel so drunk anymore. She felt alive and electrified. Her lungs powered her to get to the dim lighting of the illuminating letters spelling out "Florence Bookstore." A feeling of warmth passed through her as she remembered how often she used to go there as a kid. Too short to reach the top shelves, bugging every employee about their book opinions, even sneaking up on the bookstore cat. Those memories greeted her like an old friend. Somehow, the person she saw in the window reflection was different. But she was getting to know herself again. This was just another story she could get lost in.

A twig snapped from behind her again.

"Hello?" Wren called into the unknown.

She couldn't shake the feeling that she was being watched. She circled her surroundings, but couldn't see a soul in sight. Another twig snapped, and she whipped around. She thought she caught the faintest glimpse of blue, but it was gone in a wink. She seemed to be all alone again.

Her eyes scanned the bushes for something to take to prove that she was there. Her eye spotted a garden gnome that sat behind the bushes, too big and heavy to take. She examined it closely: the chip in its beard, the strange, crooked smile, the book it held. She eyed the gnome more closely as her fingers slid over the glasses it wore. They came right off. She smiled and continued running.

They made her stop at two other places before texting her to head to Sundae's. Her arms held the gnome's glasses, a sushi takeout menu, and a bottle of nail polish. She was in a full sprint to finish her last stop. She took a shortcut through the woods and could have sworn she saw a flash of blue again. She focused in on it, trying to catch who or what it was. It looked familiar. She smelled musky cologne in the distance that made her heart pound.

Again, it disappeared before she could get a closer look. Past the trees, Wren saw the glimmering lights from Sundae's Ice Cream Shop. Her lungs burned with excitement as she was about to finish her first dare. She dashed toward the light, and in her tipsy frenzy her foot caught something hard, launching her toward the ground. The gravel dug into her hands and hips. Her knee stung badly, and her elbows were lined with red. She looked around to see if anyone saw, or if the flash of blue would come running out to help her, but the road was empty. Everyone who was usually at Sundae's at that hour was at Grant's party. It was completely empty, Her knee flared with pain and was dripping red through her jeans.

"Great. Just great." Wren scoffed.

She whipped her head around to see what sent her plummeting to the ground. In the shadow of the dumpster, her fingers found a single brick, one that was usually used to keep the backdoor of the shop open. Wren wondered how it had made its way over by the dumpster when her phone buzzed.

There are two sides to everyone...

Valerie: grab ur souvenir and meet us under Percy Bridge, babe!

Wren checked over her injuries and assessed that she was okay to keep moving. She checked around for a souvenir, and her eyes fell again on the brick. Her fingers wrapped around it, but it was too much for her to carry. Instead, she found an empty box of waffle cones, stuffed the rest of her souvenirs in it, and set back into a jog back the way she came.

She was slightly winded by the time she met with the rest of the group. They hooted and cheered once she was in their sight. Derek immediately noticed the little splotch of blood on her pants and patched Wren's knee up with a spare bandaid in his wallet. Asa threw his arm around her, and butterflies filled her stomach. He smelled like woodsy cologne and adrenaline. She glanced at his blue shirt and the way he was also somehow trying to catch his breath.

"Were you following me?" Wren asked as Mia tossed her a White Claw.

"What? No. I've been with the group," Asa assured her, taking a sip of his drink.

Derek opened the contents of his bag, and out came cans of spray paint, masks, and gloves. Wren tossed her souvenirs in the middle of the circle. Wren was happy to see Rohit back with everyone, holding a beer in his hand, trying to mesh with the group.

Rohit tried his best to look like he was enjoying himself, trying to hide how he resented the extra company. He was used to being her partner in crime. His stomach turned and his eyes begged him to close them and go to sleep, but he saw stars in her eyes. It was the way her laugh carried that night, the way she held herself in her outfit, the way she so effortlessly completed her dare, no matter how ridiculous it was. He plastered a smile on his face anyway.

"Look at me. I'm such a bad boy." He choked a laugh, showing off his beer.

She guffawed. "Oh please, you're the furthest thing from a bad boy." Wren smiled, relieved that the night was going so well. "So where'd you go when I was running around?"

"Huh?" Rohit breathed, taking another gulp from his beer.

"You left truth or dare, remember?"

"Oh yeah. I just needed some air."

"Oh, I didn't see you outside," Wren recalled.

"Can we start already?" Mia chimed in.

Derek tossed everyone a spray can and taught them a few designs.

"You know it would have been easier for me to just send selfies, right?" Wren pointed out to the group as they painted.

"Too easy and boring. Valerie always makes people do the most," Sammy explained, nudging Valerie's shoulder.

"Be happy she wasn't in a kinky mood today. Sometimes she makes people strip." Derek laughed.

"Shut up, Derek!" Valerie shoved him hard.

"It's true though," Tyler whispered in Wren and Rohit's ears.

There are two sides to everyone...

Paint began to stretch across the bridge, making the dark underneath bright and explosively vibrant. Derek's corner was growing by the second, his artistic persona taking full control. Everyone else stuck with simple designs, trying to have the most fun with it.

Rohit drew a huge line over Wren's rose. "You asshole!" She yelled, shoving him in her all-too-familiar way. They started trying to get paint on each other and ruin each other's designs when red and blue lights flashed, the sound of car doors shutting near.

"Cops!" Tyler yelled.

"Shit! I knew we were going to get in trouble!" Rohit growled, ready to do the right thing and surrender.

"Drop the paint and RUN!" shouted Derek, leading them into the dark woods.

A clatter of fallen spray cans sputtered, and suddenly everything was in high speed. Seven pairs of shoes followed Derek through the woods, outrunning the red and blue flashing lights. They all collapsed into a heap behind the trees, heaving and sweaty, but free. The park was just as they had left it. Everything was black and blue except for a single light off the dock by the lake. Suddenly, a bright flame flickered, and the pungent scent of weed filled the air. Tyler's face was lit orange by the blunt in his hand, slowly becoming harder to see as more smoke puffed out of it. He passed it to Rohit, who took it with a shaky hand.

"Inhale, swallow, wait five seconds, exhale," Tyler instructed, leaning back to enjoy the show.

"What?" Rohit questioned, completely bewildered. "I, uh... I don't think I understand."

"Here, this might be easier," Valerie offered, taking the blunt from his hand, pressing it to her lips, and kissing him, exhaling out. Smoke smoothly moved from her lips to his, and when she let him go the smoke left his mouth as the look of utter surprise took over. "Better?"

He nodded, unsure of what to say next. Wren was bursting with excitement for her best friend. Everyone cheered and shouted with excitement as the blunt made its way around the circle along with a couple bags of chips and snacks. Wren's eyes felt heavier but good, relaxed. It was different from being drunk. Before, it felt like something in her ignited, and she was filled with energy. But this was something different. Her heart rate slowed, and her mind went to another dimension. Drugs, alcohol, a party, the police—what a night.

"I wanna go swimming," Derek announced, stripping out of his shirt and jeans and running toward the dock in his boxers.

Tyler looked back and forth from the lit blunt to the trail of clothes Derek left as he jogged in his boxers toward the water. "Me too," he chimed in, taking one last puff before following Derek's move, taking off his button down and cuffed jeans and chasing him into the moonlight.

Soon enough, everyone was running toward the lake, leaving a trail of clothes behind them. Chills ran down their arms and legs as they plunged into the water. The water echoed with laughter, and ripples swarmed their bodies in white moonlight. Weed filled the air in a cloudy daze, seducing them into a teenage dream.

Wren pulled herself out of the blue abyss, dripping in serotonin without a care in the world. She didn't even mind that she was in merely a bra and underwear because everyone else was. She dried herself off with her top, tossed it back onto the ground, and dropped down into the grass to watch the scene below. Valerie, Sammy, and Mia were playing a game of chicken on the shoulders of Tyler, Derek, and Rohit. They were giggling and screaming in playful competition as Asa's shadowy figure approached her.

"Mind if I join you?" he asked, drying himself with his shirt.

"Please." She gestured as he took up the patch of grass next to her. She was becoming more conscious of their lack of clothing. She battled with the idea of throwing her top and jeans back on.

"Having fun?"

She blinked those thoughts away. "Yes! I'm having so much fun! It's pretty much everything I've been dreaming about since I came up with the plan," Wren gushed. It was true. She was overwhelmingly happy with how everything turned out.

"And here I was, thinking that all you were dreaming about was UPenn." He smiled, his skin feeling warmer as he neared her.

"Yeah, but when goals are achieved, you make new ones. That's how you keep going."

"Always so driven." He laughed.

"You say it like it's a compliment. Before tonight, half of these guys didn't even know that my head came out of a book." Wren laughed, pointing at the rest of the group still playing in the water.

"So? What's wrong with that?" His pinky almost touched hers. She wondered if he could see the chills he gave her...

"It's boring." She whispered, nearly breathless. She had just felt a raindrop hit her leg.

"I think you're anything but boring," he whispered back honestly. And then, just like that, his hand brushed her neck and caressed her face for a moment. He pulled her close and brushed his lips against hers. He tasted of mint and cool air and got his fingers lost in her hair. He pulled her even closer, his bare chest burning against her stomach and lacy bra while her knees felt weaker. He was addictive, and she was hypnotic.

For a minute they couldn't hear anything. Not the quickening raindrops, their giggling friends, or even the water making tiny splashes. It was just them. He shivered as her fingers traced from his neck down to his back. Her stomach fluttered as he held her tighter around her waist, electrifying her every move. They were melting into each other. She brushed against his lips with something so powerful in her. Maybe it was from the adrenaline of the night or that she wanted this moment for so long or that in that exact moment, nobody expected anything of her. In that moment, Wren was enjoying herself and actually doing something that she wanted to do, not something she felt like she had to do. In that moment she felt warm, she felt happy.

She felt whole.

Chapter 12

———

There was a pounding in Wren's head, and it wasn't from the hangover wreaking havoc on her body.

Beyond the echo of steady pouring rain, the pounding continued against the house, increasing in volume. A shuffle from downstairs met the ruckus, opening the door with a squeak. Unfamiliar voices echoed through the house almost as fast as the covers were pulled off of Wren' body.

"Up. Now," Wren's mother demanded grumpily.

Wren followed her mother down the stairs, deliriously tired and aching from the night before. It felt like it had all been some wonderful fantasy. She wanted to do it again and again and find herself all over once more. Her eyes were still focusing when she finally fixed in on two figures in blue standing in the doorway amidst the hazy silhouette of the outside downpour. Suddenly, she put it together. The blue suits, the golden badges, the intense posture: they were here to arrest her for what she did last night. Maybe they hadn't outrun the cops while vandalizing the bridge. Perhaps it was a set up: catch them in the act and get them the next day. Her stomach twisted in intense pain. She wanted to throw up. She wanted to stop breathing.

"Um... good morning." Wren choked out, looking from each of the officers' badges.

"Miss Clements, we need you to come down to the station to answer some questions," the male officer ordered.

"How come? Did I do something?" Wren felt the air in her lungs leave her body, and not in a way she had ever envisioned it.

The floor began to sway beneath her feet. Her skin burned with cold sweat underneath her sweatshirt. She thought they had gotten away with it and she had successfully lived out a night in her teenage dream.

"We prefer to inform you back at the precinct," the female detective assured, her voice warmer than her partner's.

"No, you will tell us right now what's going on. She's not going anywhere with you," Wren's mother fired, her hand closing in around Wren's shoulder.

The male detective took off his sunglasses, revealing cold, dark eyes behind it. Wren's eyes flicked to his pin. It read "Moore" in black ink. Wren glanced back at the female detective. "Donovan" glinted on her pin. "This morning, a body was found near Sundae's Ice Cream Shop. The body has been identified and is known to be a classmate of your daughter's. Her name was Stella Lu."

Wren felt the whole room begin to sway, the words echoing from the detective's lips. "W-what? No, that can't be right. You have the wrong person," Wren stammered, refusing to believe anything as absurd as that. Surely this was all a dream, a nightmare, more likely.

"I'm sorry. The family has identified her. It *is* Stella," Donovan gently stated.

Sheer terror pinned her feet to the ground. Wren felt something leave her body as the horror paralyzed her to the core. *She's not dead,* Wren repeated in her mind over and over again. *She's not dead. She's not dead.*

"Oh my god. That's terrible. What happened?" Vanessa Clements questioned, rubbing her hand from Wren's shoulder to her arm.

"We'd prefer to say back at the precinct, ma'am," Donovan offered.

"What happened?" Wren croaked, surprised she could even muster out a sound.

Moore shifted his gaze from his glasses to meet Wren's eyes. "We're still investigating, but the state of Stella's injuries are severe. This was no accident. We have a killer on our hands."

Horror seized Wren's mind, soul, and everything in between as her mother held her closer. Wren had just seen Stella the day before. How had this happened? The words had to play back again in Wren's head. She was trained to absorb information instantly, but this was something new and much more difficult to swallow. She broke it apart in her head, trying to make some sense of it. A body was found. It was her classmate's.

Memories of Stella began to resurface, as if they were friends or even just barely acquaintances. That first day she met her, those times she passed her in the hallway,

Stella always marching with her nose in the air as if she were more important than everyone else. Wren's heart ached for Stella in a way she never knew that she cared.

"Jesus Christ! What's wrong with people?" Vanessa Clements gasped. "That poor girl."

"That's what we're trying to figure out as well, Mrs. Clements," Moore reassured.

"Right then. Good luck, and thank you for stopping by and notifying us." Wren's mom started to close the door when Detective Moore caught the corner with his hand, reopening it.

"Actually, Mrs. Clements, we're not here to just notify you. We need your daughter to come down to the precinct to answer some questions."

Wren's paralysis broke. Her mind was buzzing with confusion, mourning, and regret.

"What does this have to do with my daughter?" Vanessa Clements pressed, holding Wren tighter and more protective than Wren had ever seen in her life.

"Your daughter was seen leaving the scene of the crime last night," Moore replied coolly.

And then everything inside Wren exploded.

Chapter 13

Drip, drip, drip.

It had been down pouring nonstop since they left the park the previous night. Fat droplets plunged from the ceiling into a trashcan. The walls of the precinct were shrinking by the second, the gray walls careful not to let a streak of light through. Wren wanted to rip her hair out.

How could they bring her in for questioning? They said she was seen at the scene of the crime. Wren could hardly remember all the places she went the previous night. What adrenaline had pumped through her veins last night had all disintegrated into a nauseating hangover. Sludge pulsed through her body as she felt like her skin was freezing and burning at the same time. Her leg shook uncontrollably, triggering an eye roll from her mother. Wren had clearly forgotten her medicine that morning, but that was the least of her worries.

"Really? You had to sneak out *last night*?" Wren's mother hissed accusingly. "I should have never agreed to condoning this childish behavior."

Every word was like her mother twisting a knife in her side. "Mom, I really don't feel like talking right now," Wren muttered in between her stomach gurgling. Another drop from the ceiling came crashing down. Her leg trembled even more.

"Well, you better start talking. This is serious, Wren." Her mother put her hand on Wren's leg to stop it from vibrating. "They need the facts straight, so you tell them everything that happened and how they're wasting their time on you."

Her mother's voice trailed off, and Wren felt her eyes droop, the nagging feeling of exhaustion powering over her senses. She longed for her bed and to fall asleep so deeply that she would wake up and realize this was all a dream. She would see Stella the next day at school, still marching through the hallways with her nose in the air. She would shoot dirty looks at her and Asa while begging Mr. Alcott for more extra credit. She would try to run everyone over with her sickly green car and ride happily away. She would live many more years to compete against more people. She'd be alive.

"Coffee?" a woman offered, approaching Wren and her mother.

The strong punch of espresso beans filled the air, and Wren's stomach was thrown into an intense churning motion. Her leg contracted. A sharp pain pinched in her gut, and saliva filled her mouth. She felt a lurch from her insides and leapt forward, headfirst into the nearest trash can. The taste of liquor and pot deposited from her insides, leaving her gasping for air and gripping the ends of the bin tighter. Her stomach finally eased up a little more, leaving her overwhelmed body room to rest for a minute.

"I'm so sorry," she apologized to the detective whose trash can it was.

"You okay?" Wren's mother asked with a slight tone of disappointment and scolding. She had barely moved in her seat to check in on her daughter.

"Fine." She wiped her mouth. "I'm going to wash up," Wren announced, trying to scrap together what little dignity she had left, following the signs to the women's restroom.

The door creaked open, and she made her way to the sink. She turned the faucet handle to cold and cupped her hands underneath the frigid water, submerging her face in it like a brutal wakeup call. Her skin didn't feel as fiery anymore. The water snapped her back into reality as she washed away any signs of sickness. The door creaked again, but Wren was too unbothered to look and see who it was.

"Sorry about offering you the coffee," a sweet voice apologized.

Wren's head came out of the sink, dripping with cold water. The same woman who greeted her handed her a paper towel to dry off.

"Here," she said, giving Wren one more to dry her face off.

"Thank you," Wren replied through the muffled drying of her face. Her eyes started refocusing as she analyzed the woman in her twenties with cascading raven hair down her back, caramel skin, and big brown eyes. She wore a black blazer and white blouse with a pair of jeans. "It's not your fault. Must've been something I ate." Wren shrugged, hoping that her lie would suffice for her erratic behavior that morning.

"Right," the woman answered, unconvinced. "Well, I hope you're feeling better. What are you here for anyway?"

"Some detectives came to my house. They wanted me to answer some questions for an investigation. A girl I went to school with was... she was..." Wren struggled with the words for a moment. "They found her body or something." She gulped, some part of her still thinking that perhaps it wasn't true.

"That's really hard. I'm sorry." For a moment, it seemed like she wanted to reach out and give Wren a hug. "Well, if you ever find yourself here again and you're scared or nervous or just want someone to talk to, you can just ask for me. I'm Layla. Layla Nazari." She stuck her manicured hand out in front of her.

"Wren Clements." She took it and shook. "Thank you. What do you do here?" Wren rode the wave of distraction, disassociating from the news she heard that morning. She was doing what she did best: moving forward.

"I'm a detective actually. Sort of. They call me a floater. They basically give me all the shit cases that are either dead ends or too boring to solve."

"That's horrible."

"Well, there are ranks here, and I happen to be at the bottom of the totem pole. It's no biggie. Just waiting for something big to land in my lap. 'Til then, I just offer people coffee. It's just about the most interesting part of my day," she babbled. Her eyes fell upon Wren's knuckles, analyzing them as they grew whiter the more she squeezed her fingers, wringing them together. "You're gonna be okay, Wren. This is just standard procedure.

They call in people for questioning all the time for all sorts of things," she stated in an attempt to comfort her.

"Right. Okay." Wren nodded, still on edge.

Detective Nazari walked Wren back to her seat just in time for Detective Donovan to summon Wren and her mother to a private room. Wren followed her mother into what she assumed was an interrogation room. It looked just like the movies: gray walls, a huge mirror, cold air making the hairs on her skin stand up. Detective Moore was already waiting in one of the four chairs. He didn't even turn his head when the door opened.

"Please, have a seat." Detective Donovan pointed at the two chairs across from Moore.

Wren sat across from him, knowing that she was much better at reading men than she ever was with women. Sometimes they would be tougher to crack, but she always got there. Women, on the other hand, were far too complex and unpredictable. She wanted them to know she was good. She was a hardworking, studious girl bound for UPenn, certainly not a killer.

"What can you tell us about last night?" Moore started, coldly, still not making eye contact.

"What can you tell me about Stella?" Wren countered, gaining strength again.

Moore finally looked up, still unfazed, but attention caught. "Answering a question with a question. That's never a smart move."

His words hit Wren like a ton of bricks. *Must be the hangover*, thought Wren, trying to fluff her ego.

Something in her face slipped. A flinch of worry, or a flicker of fear. *Shit,* she thought.

"Answer our questions or don't answer them. I could care less." Moore tried to play it off coolly.

"You mean you *couldn't,*" Wren corrected promptly.

Detective Moore raised his eyebrows, confused by her lack of intimidation by his bad cop act.

"You *couldn't* care less. If you could care less it implies that you do care, which I think you do, considering that this is a... murder investigation," Wren explained, her voice dropping toward the end.

Moore blinked twice and then scribbled things in his notebook. That victorious feeling of proving someone wrong Wren always felt had warped into something ugly and unsettling. She regretted her know-it-all presence in that moment and wished she could rewind the last thirty seconds and start again. Things were changing, and this time they were changing for the worst.

"Wren, enough fooling around. Answer their questions and we'll be out of here in no time," her mother instructed, losing her patience with her daughter. This was not the time to be difficult.

"I can't remember a lot of it," Wren confessed. But it was the truth she had been avoiding. Since she woke that morning, pieces of her night had been scrambled or erased. She figured they would come back as the morning went on, but it was almost noon and still nothing. She was distraught.

"Miss Clements. I advise you to start remembering. Time doesn't stop when we're trying to catch a killer," Moore uttered with almost the faintest tone of a threat.

"Tell us what you do know, Wren," Donovan instructed, notepad in hand.

"She's going to UPenn in the fall," Wren's mother interjected before Wren could even open her mouth. "We need to make sure that whatever behavior took place last night," she shot an ugly glare at Wren, "won't be held against her. She'll tell you what she knows, but it stays in this room. Nothing on her record."

There were many moments in Wren's life when she didn't want her mother there, but this moment wasn't one of them. Although Vanessa was furious about Wren's absurd behavior the previous night, she still wanted what was best for her. Sure, Wren would hear a lecture about this when she got home, but in the moment, this is what Wren needed.

"We decide what gets put on her record," Moore countered, accusingly.

Wren's mother chuckled. "I'm a lawyer, Detective. You don't scare me," she challenged.

"Of course, Mrs. Clements. We understand. Your cooperation is of our utmost importance," Donovan covered. "Wren, go ahead."

Wren tried to swallow, but her throat was completely dry. She felt like she was exposing the most intimate moments of her life, but she had no choice. "Last night, I went out with a couple friends. I just wanted one night to feel… never mind. That's not the point. First, we went to the park…"

***

They escorted her out of the room about a half hour later. There was no use in keeping her if all she could remember was the park, the party, the kiss, and the most insignificant moments in between. Relief washed over Wren, making her think it was all over. She could go home, endure the scolding from her mother, and then crawl back into bed to pretend like nothing happened.

The thought wrapped around her mind like a hug. She longed to feel its safe embrace when she stumbled back into the main lobby to find a worried Derek, Mia, Sammy, Tyler, Valerie, Rohit, and Asa, all waiting to get questioned as well.

Chapter 14

"This is so fucked up," Moore muttered, tossing another crumpled paper ball at the trash can, missing it narrowly.

"Don't curse." Donovan hushed, picking up his mess, and placing it into the trash. She tried to make the best out of working with a slob.

"You and your Christian crap." Moore scoffed, checking back over his notes.

They didn't have much to work with. Wren couldn't remember much from the previous night. That was just what he needed, a suspect who couldn't remember. Or maybe she chose not to remember. His mind flicked between thoughts.

"It's not crap, Steven. And it's not because of that. A girl died. She deserves a little more than 'this is so effed up.'"

"May her soul rest in peace, blah blah. There. That doesn't help us know any more than what we currently do."

"She's in pretty bad shape."

"She's dead."

"I know, but the way they left her. It's brutal." Donovan clung to a breath she didn't realize she was holding in.

"You can't get emotional." Moore scowled, already getting annoyed with his partner.

"I'm not emotional. I'm just saying, four stab wounds and a major blow to the head is a lot for a teenage girl. What on earth happened for someone to be so cruel to her?" Donovan had a particularly hard time seeing the body that morning. It felt like she was staring at a girl who could have been her niece. She tried to choke down her feelings any time she was faced with a dead body. She knew that feminism in the workplace was all just for show, and the minute that she started revealing signs of weakness, they would have a load of paperwork waiting for her at her desk instead of the driver's seat in the patrol car.

"People are sick," Moore replied, emotionlessly.

"You really think one of these kids did it?" Donovan questioned, pacing the room.

"Those kids were caught on CCTV around town and we got that anonymous report that checks out. The odds of someone else crossing Stella's path late at night are pretty slim, especially in this town. Damn Sundae's. I've been telling them to get security cameras for years. And if this only happened earlier when there were actual customers in the store... No doubt the usual teenage crowd was also at this infamous party. If only it were a normal packed night. It would make all this shit easier. Think about how many witnesses there would be." Moore went off, despising how entangling the whole situation was.

"Part of the job, Steven. If being a detective was easy, anyone could do it," she retorted.

"I think we've already reached that point," Moore muttered under his breath.

Donovan heard it anyway. Her mind ran through all the different situations. She could easily tell him off, but where would that get her? Probably riding the desk for a while. This investigation was too important to her. It would be good for her career, and she owed it to herself to at least not go down without a fighting chance. She merely let the rude words her partner always seemed to mutter roll off her back. The biggest strength was to not give it the power to hurt her. Instead, she popped her head through the door to the hallway. "Ready for the next one."

A sweet looking girl stepped into the room. She had caramel skin and dressed in a blue cap sleeve dress. She looked terribly out of place as she took a seat in the cold metal chair.

"Miss Valerie Scott, I presume?" Moore questioned glumly.

Valerie nodded until she realized that Moore wasn't making eye contact. "Yes... sir."

"Honey, what can you tell us about last night?" Donovan began, taking over the reins of the interrogation.

"There was a party. Basically the whole school was there."

"Was Stella Lu there?"

"What? No. She... I mean, she wasn't really the party type. She never went to any parties. She was always very studious..." Valerie thought about how Stella might react to being talked about in that way. "That's an understatement. She was a genius," she corrected. Valerie filled her lungs with a deep inhale. She choked back tears. "I can't believe she's gone. What happened to her?"

"But then you left at some point." Donovan changed the subject as Moore continued to scribble in his notebook.

"Huh?"

"The party. You left at some point."

"Y-yes. We were just walking around afterward. Goofing around," Valerie replied through tight lips.

"Miss Scott, you should know that we're not here to arrest you for being drunk and disorderly. We just want to get some facts straight to get a feel if anyone saw anything of more value," Donovan explained.

"Why didn't they let Wren talk to us?" Valerie countered, changing the subject. It had rubbed her the wrong way how those officers rushed her out of the precinct faster than Wren could even get a word out to her friends. "Those cops escorted her out as if she was guilty."

"She could be guilty." Moore broke his silence.

"You can't be serious." Valerie scoffed in disbelief.

"We're just trying to get the facts straight. No one is throwing any sort of accusations around," Donovan assured Valerie while shooting a death glare back at her partner.

"With all due respect, you guys have to do a better job than this. We were with each other all night. There's no way any of us could have done something to Stella. She was our classmate, for god's sake! Yeah, we went out the same night. But we never even saw her."

Time was a crucial factor when it came to solving this crime. If it weren't for the rain the previous night leading into the morning, the detectives wouldn't have felt like they were at such a loss. It was going to be much harder to find Stella's exact time of death. Any sort of DNA evidence would have been drowned in the puddles of the parking lot and long gone. Officers and forensics were working tirelessly at the scene of the crime, trying to scrape up anything that hadn't been washed away. They were hoping to find some sort of lead, anything at all to help them find who killed her.

For now, this gang of teens was all they had. Hopefully, that would be enough to catch a killer.

***

"So what happened at this party?" Donovan pressed, firing through the same questions she gave the others.

"Not a fucking murder, if that's what you're asking," Mia fired back. She was repulsed by the very room she was in. It was a horrible way to spend her Saturday. She would have much rather preferred to be in her boyfriend's shirt, on his couch, watching reruns of *I Love Lucy.*

"I understand that you're upset. You lost a classmate." Donovan tried to make sense of her reaction. Moore continued to scribble vigorously in his notebook.

"Honestly, I don't really care about Stella. This is a fucking waste of time." Mia rolled her eyes.

"Some would say that a murder investigation isn't a waste of time. It's actually quite productive," Donovan defended herself. Something about Mia made her feel uneasy. Her attitude made Donovan feel like she had something to prove. She always had something to prove.

"Whatever." Mia snorted.

"Tell the nice lady what she wants to hear before *I* start asking. And trust me, I'm not as pleasant to talk to," Moore interrupted, lifting his eyes from his notepad just enough to give Mia a chastising glare.

"Dancing, beer pong, Valerie's famous truth or dare. The normal stuff."

"And did everyone like that stuff? Were there any problems at the party?"

"No…" Mia started. But then she began to remember. "But there was someone who got pretty upset during truth or dare."

***

Rohit Kumar looked like he would rather pass away than be in the interrogation room with two detectives and his mother.

"So we hear you got pretty upset during truth or dare," Donovan pointed out.

"*Truth or dare.*" Rohit's mother scoffed. "What truth? This boy can't be truthful at all apparently."

"Mrs. Kumar, we would really appreciate it if you let your son answer our questions."

There are two sides to everyone…

"Well, let me tell you. This behavior is completely out of sorts. I spend my whole life, raising him to get good grades, make good and rational decisions, and this is where we end up. This is what happens when you don't listen to me, Rohit. Do you want to go to jail?" Mrs. Kumar's eyes had a certain power over Rohit. She could make him shrink into a corner begging for forgiveness in a single glare.

"Mrs. Kumar, please? Rohit isn't in trouble. We are just asking him some questions to get our story straight." Donovan persisted.

"My apologies, detective." She cooperated, and then she shot her son another glance. "We'll continue this discussion at home," she whispered, trying to bite her tongue before she found more things to yell at him about.

"Rohit, what happened at truth or dare?"

A million things were whirling through Rohit's mind. Stella. How Brown would want to revoke his acceptance after this. The police. Wren. His parents. His sister. School. Stella. Stella. Stella. He shifted in his chair and felt himself clenching his fingers around the arms.

"It was just a normal game of truth or dare," Rohit explained, fearful for everything in his life that was now on the line.

"That's not what others are saying. Mia mentioned that you left in the middle of the game."

"I came back."

"Why did you leave? When did you leave?" Donovan grilled.

"I don't remember what time it was. Maybe a little past midnight? I just needed some air," Rohit confessed.

"You *just* needed air? Mia made it sound like you were upset about something."

Fuck Mia, thought Rohit. He knew that once the cops had something in their mind, they wouldn't let it go. They needed to know all the facts. The feeling was familiar to Rohit. With a deep sigh, he knew he would regret opening his mouth. "I *was* upset." No turning back now. "Because Wren likes Asa."

The moment it left his lips, he knew he wouldn't hear the end of it when he got home. He would become the disgrace of his family. Everything that he had worked for would go to shit because of a girl. *The* girl.

"Thank you for coming in, Rohit. We'll be in touch with any follow up questions. We appreciate your cooperation," Donovan thanked him.

Moore simply continued to scribble into his notepad.

There are two sides to everyone...

Chapter 15

———

"You're a good detective, but I would really appreciate it if you could act a little bit interested in this investigation." Donovan muttered between sips of her coffee.

"Most partners would be happy that they have someone to play 'good cop, bad cop' with. Doing you a favor, Donovan." Moore cooly replied, still scribbling on his paper.

Donovan knew better than anybody else that Detective Steven Moore didn't have to *play* bad cop—that's who he was. Probably one of those entitled pricks who grew up thinking they could be the main character of every cop movie. But who was going to do the heavy lifting? Who was going to help the main character crack the case? The side characters. That's why he had more arrests than her. She did the heavy lifting, and she was quickly trying to get over that. "Stop scribbling in that damn thing."

Moore lifted his head, eyes wide with surprise. "You cursed. You never curse."

"Your bad attitude is rubbing off on me," she said, glumly.

"Good. One step closer to being a real cop, sweetheart." Moore chewed on his pen.

Something in Donovan's stomach twisted, and she had to turn and look at the door to hide her scowl. She felt her fingers close around the door handle and a foot slip out the door. She caught herself wondering why she hadn't decided to become a schoolteacher or a dancer or any other female dominated field. She resented those moments. It made her weak. It made her want to fight for her spot that much more. She pulled her foot back inside and instead popped her head out, calling for the next person to come in and answer her questions.

They had already interviewed Sammy Rodriguez and Derek Sanders in the last hour. The pair had been no help. They didn't see anything suspicious, nor did they think anything of the investigation. Sammy had said "Maybe it was some freak accident." Donovan had nodded simply at that. *If only it were a simple accident*, she thought to herself. Donovan felt as though perhaps it wasn't best to tell these teenagers just how brutally Stella was injured and how she was left for dead in the same place she had probably gone to get ice cream for years. *Some freak accident*, thought Donovan as Tyler Harrison walked through the doorway.

"Please, have a seat."

He did as he was told. He was less shaky than the others. There was much more time for the news to sink in. It had been about three hours since they had summoned everyone to the precinct for questioning.

"Thank you for your patience."

"Of course," Tyler offered.

Donovan was taken aback by his attitude. He was sweeter than the others. Very polite. She wished everyone who ended up in that room was like him. She analyzed him in his flannel and band tee with jeans folded over at the ankles. They were wrinkled and probably unwashed, but somehow suited him and his untidy dark hair.

"How are you doing?"

"A little hungover, but I'll live." He smiled. It drooped a little when he realized how it had come out. He wished he could take it back and answer again, this time more professional. "Sorry. That was insensitive."

Donovan tried to hide the smile that was building in the corner of her lips. She was grateful for his honesty. Candor wasn't something she had come across often, especially with teenagers. She felt a release in her core. She wouldn't have to try as hard for this interrogation.

"Here. Drink some water," Donovan advised, passing him a sealed bottle on the table. "Were you close with the victim?"

"No. To be honest, we all kind of didn't get along."

"Who is 'we all'?"

"Everyone who goes to school with us. I'm sure Stella was a great person once you *really* got to know her, but that's the thing. She was never interested in people really getting to know her. She wouldn't even be friends with Wren and Rohit, which was kind of odd because they're so similar." Tyler explained before taking a large gulp from the bottle.

"They're similar? How?" Donovan questioned, pulling her hair behind her ear as if she needed it there to hear better.

"They're, like, the top of our class. Rohit is valedictorian, Wren is salutatorian, and Stella was next. If you ask me, Stella was always trying to catch up. It's a shame that Wren and Stella hated each other." He took another sip before realizing how cruel that sounded. How could he have been so stupid, to make such statements during a murder investigation? "I'm sorry. They didn't hate each other. They just didn't get al... see eye to eye. They didn't see eye to eye. That's why they stayed away from each other."

"I see. And did Wren ever tell you anything about Stella? Was there something more than rivalry?" Donovan pressed, eager to find a shred of a lead.

"No. It's not what you think, trust me. Even though they were similar, they were still really different. Wren wanted more than good grades. That's why we went out last night. Trust me, there were a million other things on her mind last night." He assured, nervously.

Donovan could hear Tyler's voice getting more defensive. If she was going to get these teenagers to trust her, she needed to tread lightly. He seemed very convinced that Wren had nothing to do with it. "Okay, thank you. Moving on: We've been taking statements from everyone about what they saw, what happened at this party, and anything out of the ordinary."

Tyler took a big gulp of water. "Right. It was pretty much a normal party."

"So we've heard," Moore chimed in.

"We heard there were some issues with truth or dare," Donovan offered, hoping to gain another perspective.

There are two sides to everyone...

"Oh, Asa? Well, he told me not to tell anybody. I don't know how the others found out."

That was not what Donovan was expecting to hear at all. She checked her file. Asa Mitchell had yet to be questioned. "Sorry, Tyler. Could you clarify? Found out about what?"

"Asa left the party a little after Wren left to complete her dare."

"Right, the dare. And when was this?"

"Around midnight, I think."

"Midnight. Everyone goes fucking missing around midnight," Moore muttered, tossing his notepad down on the table.

Donovan caught a glimpse of what was scribbled on it. It looked like grids and lines, merely etched with fading ink. Thank goodness she was recording the conversation.

***

"So, we hear that you also went out around midnight," Donovan stated.

"I did. But it's not what you think," Asa begged, already with a tone of apology shaking in his voice. Asa had been raised by a single mother who grew up in Philadelphia. She was from Kensington and miraculously climbed her way out of poverty and crime and ended up in the suburbs. She was intelligent from a young age and had learned to keep her head down. Those were the same survival tools she had bestowed to her son. Be good, be smart, and never get in trouble with the law. Had he only listened to the first two parts, perhaps he wouldn't have found himself leaving the party at midnight in a hurry. Perhaps he wouldn't have found himself sitting in that freezing room staring at two strangers questioning his whereabouts as if he was a suspect.

"And what do we think?" Donovan pressed, leaning forward. Even Moore had taken interest, eyes up, staring at what might lead to a huge break in the case.

"That I saw something last night. But I didn't. Valerie is famous at school for giving crazy dares. It was Wren and Rohit's first night, so she was going easy on them. She dared Wren to go on some nighttime scavenger hunt around town, but it was late. Everyone was really drunk, so they didn't think there was anything wrong with it. I just couldn't let her go out on her own. If something had happened to her..." The thought entered his mind, sending a shiver down his spine. "I knew I had to keep an eye out for her from a distance. I didn't want anyone to know because, well... Wren's super tough. She isn't someone who needs looking after. I just wanted to." The memories came flooding back as they left his lips. She was drunkenly running all over town. He had been to enough parties before in which the same situation would end in an arrest. He lurked by the trees, careful to keep up with her anytime she switched locations. He almost blew his cover multiple times, but he managed to keep sinking in with his shadow in the woods. He watched as her thick ponytail came thrashing behind her and how she ran so freely and elegantly through the night. She was remarkably gifted at everything she did. She didn't need saving. He knew she could handle herself if anything serious happened, but he wouldn't be able to sit still at the party, not knowing if she was okay. "I left once she got to Sundae's. Val sent a text to meet up, and I wanted to get there before Wren so she wouldn't know I was following her."

"And did anyone see you? Anyone to vouch for where you were when you said you were gone?" Donovan questioned, sure to not rule out any suspects.

"I don't think so, but I have a GPS app on my phone. My mom uses it in case of emergencies," Asa offered, pulling out his phone.

"We'll take a look at it soon," Donovan replied, studying his face. He had deep skin and chocolate eyes. Honest. Good. "Did you see anyone or anything suspicious?"

"No. It was just a normal night. It was quiet besides everyone from the party. I wish I would have seen something to help. I can't believe what happened to Stella." Asa had never fully warmed up to Stella. She was always caught up in her own agenda, but no one deserved to die so young. He was sorry he never really got the chance to know her. He hated how he never thought about her while she was alive. Perhaps this is what happens when someone dies. They suddenly occupy every inch of your mind, and you begin to despise yourself for not giving them a chance... for not giving a shit until they were gone.

"So you weren't close?"

"No. Stella wasn't really close to anyone," Asa replied, sorry that she had to go through life that lonely.

"Well, clearly someone was," Moore pointed out before scribbling more into his notebook.

Chapter 16

"How could you be so stupid?"

Wren's mother belittled her the whole way home while finding fault with the detectives at the same time. Wren was getting tired of it. She needed to sleep. Or maybe she needed to wake up and discover that this was all a horrible dream. Stella would be alive, her friends wouldn't have been dragged in for questioning, and she could be kissing Asa all over again.

In a blink, she was transported back to laying in the grass, soaking wet from jumping in the lake, feeling goosebumps tickle down her bare spine. Then she felt warmth and an explosion of euphoria when he got close to her and brushed his fingertips along her cheek. He tasted like mint candy and made her body alive. And now everything had fallen to shit.

She prayed to whatever god was up there that this morning was just a horrible dream.

"Look at me when I'm talking to you," Wren's mother commanded, pulling into their driveway. She was livid, already being dragged into the police station and then having to go around town buying some supplies to cure Wren's hangover. A part of her wanted her daughter to suffer a little and stew in her failure.

Wren urged every muscle in her body to turn her head toward her mother. How could Wren face her after being a complete and utter disappointment? Her fingers subtly reached past the hem of her pants to feel three thin slits across her skin. How easy it would be to hop into the hot shower and leave all these emotions to drain away. Every nerve in her body cried for a release.

"Wren!"

Wren's head flipped toward her mother so fast that it triggered another headache. "I'm sorry."

"'I'm sorry' isn't going to fix this, Wren. You snuck out and drank and god knows what else! You have a duty to this family. Do you know that?" her mother fired back.

"Yes."

"What is it?" she barked.

"To be perfect," Wren said, just above a whisper.

"So much for that," her mother snapped, opening the car door and heading into the house.

Wren followed her inside, scared for what was to come. She lingered by her office, feeling like a stranger in the threshold. Her mother's office was piled high with paperwork, and despite the rest of the house being in pristine condition, this room was the one drowning in work. Her mother sifted through stacks of papers and sat down with a file at her desk.

"So what do we do now?" Wren asked, nervous for what repercussions dared to threaten her and her family.

"Well, they'd be ridiculous to come after a minor. What, like there aren't hundreds of other kids in this town who were out partying? They've got it coming if they think about labeling you as a prime suspect," her mother listed, still engrossed in her paperwork.

Wren was still trying to catch her breath. *Prime suspect*? How could they possibly think that? Did she really raise that many red flags? Wasn't there any way that this had all just been a strange coincidence and she could mourn Stella's death without feeling a noose slowly tighten around her neck? Wren was spiraling. Was it all worth it? Why couldn't she enjoy one night without any sort of consequences. Why was this happening? Her body trembled with the fear of the unknown.

"So, will you defend me if something happens?" Wren whispered, hoping her mother would still look out for her.

Her mother looked up with worried eyes. A deafening silence hung in the air as she ran through a million situations in her head. She hoped it wasn't true. It couldn't be... "Wren, did you..."

"No! God, Mom, no! Absolutely not." Wren's eyes filled with tears at the mere thought of poor Stella's lifeless body. "How could you think that I..." Wren choked the tears back before they started to stream down her cheeks. "I didn't do it."

Mrs. Clements rushed over with relief growing in her chest and wrapped her arms around her daughter uncomfortably. It felt foreign, but it was necessary. She held her daughter there for a moment or two before letting go. "Of course. I didn't think that, but I just had to make sure. You're my daughter. I have to have your back."

The words sounded as if it were coming out of someone else's mouth. Wren took a step back at the fact that she may have accidentally discovered her mother's heart. She wiped a tear that tried to slip out. "So, what do we do now?"

"Well, *you* are going to lay low. Act how you normally do. Don't give the police a reason to suspect you." Her mother tucked a lock of hair behind Wren's ear. "And don't ever pull a stunt like last night again," she threatened through clenched teeth.

Wren nodded her head as her heart dropped ten stories. The closest Wren's ever felt to herself was what she had felt last night. It was the person who was able to let go and live in the moment that she loved. Perhaps she would never be able to see her again. Perhaps the version of herself she's always known was safe and reliable and the closest to perfect that she would ever be.

***

Wren needed her best friend and that's how she found herself an hour later throwing tiny pebbles at Rohit's window. She rang his doorbell, but no one answered. She even texted him, but Wren had suspected that his mother took his phone away. Rohit was always telling her about how Indian parents were a completely different level of strict. One time in third grade Rohit got a 90 percent on a math test, and his parents banned him from watching television for a month.

Suddenly, a shadow passed in the room and Wren saw Rohit's frame in the window. She gestured for him to come down and meet her in his backyard. The back of his house faced the woods, and they could easily sink behind the trees undetected. Wren didn't want to risk Rohit getting punished even more. She waited beside a large tree trunk, hoping that he would be brave enough to come outside. She needed to talk to him about everything. She needed her best friend to tell her that everything was going to be okay and she was just anxious about the investigation. She needed him to understand exactly what it was that she was feeling. Minutes drifted by in the cool night air, and just when she was ready to turn back and go home she heard a shuffle in the grass. She waited for Rohit to meet her eyes, but to her surprise she was greeted by Ria, his sister.

"Ria! How are you? Are your parents freaking out like mine are? Oh god, this is such a mess." Wren babbled nervously, trying to get some of the weight off of her chest. Her eyes caught the moment Ria's gaze changed. Eyes that were always excited to see Wren were filled with regret. "What's wrong? Where's Ro?"

"He doesn't want to see you right now," Ria muttered painfully.

Wren felt like she had the wind knocked out of her. Clearly, she didn't hear her correctly. "What? You're joking." Never once in their years of friendship had Rohit not wanted to see her. He was as important to her as the blood that pumped through her veins. He was more family than what she lived with back home. He was always there for her. Always. She didn't know how she was supposed to go on without him.

"Well, he wants to, but he can't. My mom is... well, she's not really saying good things about you right now. She doesn't think it's good for us to be around you." Ria's voice got shakier as she neared the end. She reverted her eyes down to her shoes, shame building in her stance.

"I thought your mom loved me." Wren breathed, taking the words in like she had been slapped across the face. "Why does she think that?"

"Because Rohit told her that sneaking out was your idea all along and you forced him into it."

Her words hit Wren like a ton of bricks. "That's bullshit. He wanted to go too." Wren tried to look back up at the house to see if Rohit was there and he would just come and talk to her and tell her it wasn't true.

"I believe you, Wren. But now isn't the best time. I'm really sorry." And with that, she ran back to her house. At least she had the guts to say it to Wren's face. At least Ria thought Wren deserved better than a mere glance through a bedroom window.

With their porch light flicking off, Wren felt more alone than ever in the darkness of the night. She was hyperventilating on feelings that she wanted nothing to do with. Her life was being derailed by something she had no business with, and now even her best friend had turned his back on her.

Wren walked home with tears brimming in her eyes and a knot tightening in her chest. She thought about going to a million different places, but instead found herself in the shower with a razor in hand. The hot water made her skin red as she sliced away every emotion she was feeling.

And down the drain they went.

Chapter 17

___

Wren's mind was going in circles.

It never took her this long to understand things, but then again, nothing was as it used to be anymore.

She clutched her knees closer to her chest, hoping to find some form of warmth in a dark world. She couldn't bring herself to lay in the comfort of her bed or sit in a chair. She yearned for feeling as bad as she did on the inside. The mahogany floor laid unwelcoming as she curled up on her side, willing her eyes to look anywhere but her phone.

> *Valerie: i still can't believe what happened to stella*
>
> *Tyler: its crazy*
>
> *Derek: i feel like i should have known her. yk, before*
>
> *Sammy: before she died. yeah, me 2*
>
> *Wren: I did know her. It's worst when you know them.*

Wren had spent hours running through her memories. Death was foreign and all the more jarring. It was like every memory of Stella wasn't real and was in some old Hollywood black and white film. Flamboyantly raising

There are two sides to everyone...

her hand in class just to show off, zooming through the parking lot without a care in the world—it was all distant. Wren questioned if Stella had always been a ghost or if Wren was just too competitive to realize that Stella was more than just the competition. She was the motivation. She pushed Wren and therefore was an angel in disguise. She didn't even know it.

Wren had a particularly hard time grasping loss. Her brain felt broken, like some curious unsolvable problem, and she felt more empty inside than she had ever felt. There were too many things on her mind: Stella, Rohit, Asa, the killer, the investigation. It all wrapped itself into one nauseating experience.

Her eyes filled with salty water, but she didn't dare let it fall. She had been trying to gain better control over her emotions. The cut on her side stung like a punishment. It didn't fill the emptiness inside. It didn't even suffice as her normal release. It was just another cut on her side to remind her that just about everything in her life was so tragically messed up and there was nothing in her control.

Mia: this whole investigation is bullshit

Sammy: its not bullshit Mia they're doing their job

Tyler: yeah by asking us if we had anything to do with it

Asa: this is all so fucked up.

*Valerie: ^^*

Derek: they're really acting like they never heard of parties before. shit happens.

Asa: not a murder investigation

Wren: And definitely not being seen where she was found.

Tyler: they'd have to be dumb to think it's u

Mia: just bc u guys hated each other doesn't mean u have some murder lust

If Wren was going to wrangle in her emotions, she would need to stop thinking like a teenage girl who just got brought in for questioning and instead put herself in someone else's shoes. Wren thought about what the detectives would be thinking. They would evaluate the scene and assess what they already knew. An eighteen-year-old girl named Stella Lu was killed and left for dead near the dumpsters at Sundae's Ice Cream Shop. Teenagers were all over town, drunkenly walking about, but only one was seen at the scene of the crime. She had minimal recollection of events, was drunk out of her mind, and saw no one else. She rejoined her friends at the end of her dare and lived through the rest of the night. She lived for another day while the other lay rotting for dead. Stella hated a lot of people, but Wren was the only one everyone knew of. Unless there was someone else. There had to be. *Someone* killed that poor girl.

They would probably spend the next few days going through phone records, credit card bills, and email exchanges to see if there was any more information they could learn about her.

For now, Wren would have to sit still and lay low like her mother told her. There was nothing she could do but hope that they would catch the killer quickly. It would put a stop to everything. Stella would get justice, Rohit would talk to her again, and she wouldn't be questioned like she was the prime suspect.

Despite having nothing to do with it, she still felt blood on her hands. She felt responsible, and in a gut-wrenching epiphany she knew why she felt so wounded that she couldn't even get up. It was Rohit and the way he blamed her for everything that happened.

He doesn't want to see you right now.

Ria's voice echoed through her mind every time it went blank. Those words had felt like a knife in her side. How had those words hurt her more than anything she had ever felt? How could he do that to her? Had she ever really known him at all?

Of course she had. Rohit was her best friend. He was always going on about how strict his traditional Indian parents were, so surely this was related. But why hadn't he texted or called or even tried to see how she was holding up? Had he really cared that little for her? Was he so ready to throw years of friendship, trust, and loyalty down the drain? All of it must have been an act to appease his mother, surely. There was no way that he could have Ria say those things and mean it. There was just no way.

Wren had to stop herself before her eyes let a tear slip out. She was upset how easily her emotions took over, as if everything she had worked toward had been undone by a little salt water. She was trying to not give it the power to upset her even more. A buzz sounded from her phone, and she fed into the distraction.

Asa: can we talk?

Wren: yeah

Asa: pick you up in 10

Wren was shocked to find her heart still flutter, given everything that had happened. It seemed to be the only part of her still intact, and she clung to it as she unraveled herself from the fetal position and stood up. She took a long look at her reflection in the mirror. She had been curled up in a UPenn sweatshirt and shorts and had her hair up in a messy bun. This was the best it was going to be at the moment.

Minutes felt like seconds as Asa pulled into her driveway in a blink. His shoulders tensed up as she sat down next to him. Wren tried to distract herself by the road. There weren't many cars out at the time, but a black truck with dark windows followed about thirty feet behind. Asa drove them to the park while silence hung in the air. Wren recognized the places that she and Rohit used to sit and talk for hours. The spots that had the perfect amount of sunlight and the places that got too muddy when it rained the day before. She had a sudden aching to be there with Rohit and to hope that all was forgiven. But she did nothing that needed to be forgiven. It wasn't her fault. Why did everyone think it was her fault?

"Wren." Asa finally spoke. He reached over to fit her hand in his with a squeeze. "Are you okay?"

Her fingers started to warm up, intertwined with his. She wanted to say yes, but "No."

"I know." He nodded, pulling her in for a warm embrace.

"Are *you* okay?" she asked, voice muffled in his shoulder.

"No." He sighed, and they hugged tighter.

Time didn't stop this time. Things were different, and Wren could feel it. He left her arms and rested his back on his seat. "Wren, I don't want to sound insensitive, especially with all the shit going on. I know it's not your fault, but…"

There are two sides to everyone…

There it was. It hung in the air like that A– in AP Econ. It was so close to being something nice, but was just the opposite of that. She dreaded what she had to ask next.

"But what?"

"This investigation is really hard to deal with."

"I know," Wren whispered, terrified that she might lose him too.

"I know you know. But you know that I'm not the same as you." His chocolate eyes focused on hers.

"I know, Asa."

"My mom grew up in Philly in one of the worst neighborhoods. She moved out here to get away from the crime and craziness. She didn't want me to go through all that. When they called me into that room and asked me questions... I don't know. It just didn't feel great. And now you know that, it's just... Based on the stories m told me from her childhood, I just never thought that I would end up in a room like that. It feels like I kind of let her down."

Asa was right. She would never know what it feels like to be him. She didn't want him to go through that anymore. Maybe if she let him go, it would be easier than when Rohit refused to talk to her. It wouldn't hurt as much if she would just cut him loose and things were to end on her terms. "I get it, Asa. It's okay, you don't have to see me again." She shrugged, getting out of the car before he could say anything else.

"Wait, Wren!" Asa jumped out from his door and looped around to her side. "Who said that I don't want to see you again?"

Her back was against the car and his hands were placed on each side of the door, keeping her in place. "Look, you don't have to pretend you like me anymore, Asa. Things have changed. I get it. This is all so fucked up. Stella's gone, and Rohit won't even talk to me. I'm a suspect in a murder investigation..."

"Rohit won't talk to you?"

"No. Something about this being all my fault," Wren muttered. "He had his sister deliver the news. It was a real dick move."

Asa lifted a hand to her face and affectionately tucked a lock of hair behind her ear. He then took both his hands on either side of her face, locking his eyes completely with hers. "Listen to me, Wren. This is not your fault. They are unusual circumstances, and we happened to be at the wrong place at the wrong time."

"I knew you were trailing me in the woods when I did that dare. I saw your shirt a few times and figured it was you," she explained, seeing his eyes widen at her observation. "You didn't have to follow me that night. I didn't need you there. I can handle myself," Wren explained, knowing that he wouldn't be entangled in her mess if he had just stayed with the others at the party.

"I know you can," he said just before he brushed his lips against hers. It was different and felt real. It was innocent and unhazy. He felt even more alive than when they first kissed. There was power and it was raw, like something deep down inside of them had surfaced, wonderfully understood.

Wren was ecstatic to see that he still had feelings for her. Even though they had been through an extreme

There are two sides to everyone...

event, he was going to be there no matter what. He leaned in to kiss her again before something dark caught Wren's eye.

"What's wrong?" Asa questioned, dying to shut her up with his lips.

"That truck." Wren gestured with her head. "I saw it when we were coming here. I didn't see anyone get out."

"Maybe they're waiting for somebody," Asa offered.

Wren squinted her eyes, trying to see through the tinted windows. Just then, the engine started up and launched the car in forward, zooming past them into the street and out of sight.

Chapter 18

Sunday went by in a blink. Still following her mother's directions of staying out of sight, Wren didn't leave the house, even for something as small as checking the mail. That truck that was trailing her and Asa hadn't left her mind. She felt like she ran the risk of being followed if she went out on her own again. Wren even contemplated if school was where she wanted to be, but her mother assured her that things would only work out if she didn't draw attention to herself.

A journalist had written an article in the local newspaper. Stella's murder was everywhere now. She had been stabbed four times and had a major blow to her head. She died some point between midnight and three in the morning. Her parents said that she left the house around 11:30 p.m. and she never came home. They didn't know where she was until she was found.

Before Wren knew it, it was Monday morning, and the whole school was buzzing over the weekend news. Announcements over the intercom were offering counseling services instead of advertising bake sales. It was the

There are two sides to everyone…

type of topic that everyone couldn't help talking about but somehow felt guilty for discussing it. There was chatter on every corner, whispers in passing, the deafening silence of serious conversation dominating the halls...

"Wren, over here," Tyler called from his locker. She noticed everyone was standing there waiting for her. Everyone except for Rohit.

Wren glanced over at Rohit unzipping his backpack in the corner. There he was, in his normal smart casual outfit, putting his books away. He checked his phone, causing Wren's blood to boil. His mom didn't take his phone away after all—he was purposefully avoiding her. That asshole had his phone the whole time while Wren kept texting him, begging him to talk to her, and it was like he didn't even care. How could he be that cruel? Wren felt the knot in her chest tighten, as if it could have tightened any more.

"Wren, you okay?" Asa asked, lacing his hand in hers like it belonged there the whole time.

"Yeah." Wren blinked away any signs of distress. "I'm good."

Asa led her to the rest of the gang. They, like the rest of the school, were in deep conversation, talking about the series of events that weekend.

"I heard that Isaac Reed was the one who found her," Sammy whispered.

"Relax, Sammy. He's not here. You don't have to whisper," Derek pointed out.

"Dude, it's not cool to talk about that stuff so openly. Could you imagine what he's going through right now?" Tyler fired back. "Someone died. Show some compassion."

"Sorry."

"I think we *should* talk about this," Mia interjected.

Everyone stared, shocked at Mia. Everyone but Wren, who tried to seem as emotionless as possible. She didn't need any eyes drawn to her. She was laying low, and she was going to get through this day, and then the next, and the next after that.

"Could you guys not look at me like I'm crazy?" Mia exclaimed with fire in her voice.

"Mia, what good will that do? Talking about it will just upset people, especially because we were all called in for questioning," Valerie explained. She was dressed down, in a Valerie way. Her hair was in a ponytail, and she was wearing a short black dress. Her nails had been bitten raw. It was clear this investigation was getting to her too.

"Will anyone be *that* upset? This is Stella we're talking about," Mia stated nonchalantly.

"Mia!" Everyone practically shouted in unison.

"I think she might be right," Wren finally whispered. Everyone's heads turned her way. "Look, someone is responsible for this. Right now, I'm the best lead that they've got." The gears had been turning in her head the night before. This was the only way she was ever going to be okay. "Maybe someone here knows something. Stella basically lived at school. There has to be something here that we can find out."

"So what? We're supposed to take this investigation into our own hands now?" Derek questioned, unconvinced.

"Wren, I think we should leave the investigating to the detectives," Asa advised.

"You know more than anyone that they're looking at the wrong person," Wren said with a blank stare. She was wrangling her emotions and was going to be focused today. She had to be if she wanted out of this mess. There was no time to feel.

"Okay, Wren. I'll keep an eye out," Tyler offered, giving her shoulder a squeeze.

The bell rang for first period, and the mob in the hallway dispersed into different ends of the school.

"Wren." Asa squeezed her hand. "It'll be okay."

Wren found her head nodding as she unlaced her fingers and made her way to first period.

It would be okay. This was what she was good at. She always needed to know the answers. However, in this case, it wasn't just an answer to a calculus problem. She had to find who was responsible. Her shoulders felt heavier as she sat in class. Her breathing intensified. She was exploding on the inside, but didn't dare move a muscle. She let the whispers roll off her back. She didn't engage. She just listened and observed, hoping to come across something that would lead her in any sort of direction.

She had heard all sorts of absurd things that day.

"Stella took her spot at UPenn. Then Wren got all crazy and killed her. Good luck with college now," someone whispered in class.

"Jesus, these smart kids are fucking nuts."

"That's not true. I feel like Stella had it coming after she started that rumor about Wren's ADHD," another one added.

Wren's skin stung a little after hearing this. She thought everyone forgot about the ridiculous rumor. She had certainly tried to move on from that incident. It was just another thing to remind her how far from perfect she was.

The only thing that got her to AP Econ was knowing that Asa would be there and she wouldn't have to be alone with her thoughts again. The weight from her shoulders seemed to ease up when she walked through the door and looked over at his tall frame. Then her eyes fell on the empty desk at the front, and her body instantly tightened again.

"It's okay, Wren," Asa whispered, gesturing for her to take her seat.

She sat behind him, and he let his hand reach for hers and interlace with her fingers. Her heart gave a flutter at how easily he was able to make her feel safe. It felt like, for once, she didn't have to keep her thoughts to herself. He knew her in a way that Rohit didn't. Maybe he knew her better than Rohit ever did. Asa didn't leave her when things got tough.

"Okay, class. As many of you know, we lost a student over the weekend. The school wants me to remind you that you are more than welcome to leave and go to the counselor if you are upset. If not, I'm sure Stella would want us all to continue with our classwork," Mr. Alcott announced dryly, handing papers out.

Everyone groaned. The whole day had been filled with movie watching or silent reading, but of course Mr. Alcott had more work for them to do. Only he would be indifferent in an intense situation.

The rest of the class seemed to fall away as Wren and Asa worked on their classwork silently. Asa didn't even say anything when Wren got a question wrong. Everything seemed to shift back into place until the door opened with a squeak and a pair of heavy shoes stomped inside. Everyone's eyes rose from their papers to the doorway, finding a large man in a dark blue police officer's uniform. He whispered something to Mr. Alcott before he nodded his head and his dark eyes met Wren's.

"Wren. Your presence is requested elsewhere. I'm sure Mr. Mitchell will catch you up on what you missed later." Mr. Alcott spoke as if it was completely normal for a police officer to interrupt class to question one of his students.

Wren felt a pulse from Asa' s hand to hers as his eyes said it all. *It'll be okay.*

She inhaled and put her books back in her bag, and she carried herself and her things out of the room with extreme composure. Voices began whispering the second she passed through the doorway, but the door slammed, leaving her out of the loop again.

"Can I ask what this is about?" Wren questioned, already following the officer down the halls.

"We just need you to come back to the station and answer some more questions," the officer replied in a booming voice.

There was something in the air that felt like impending doom. Wren's own clothes made her skin feel uncomfortable, and she found herself wanting to stop time and run away. She sat silently in the uncomfortably rigid backseat of the police car the whole ride there. Her mind was bombarding her with debates over her innocence and what the detectives were thinking of. The minute she stepped inside the precinct, the room began to sway. The grays of the walls seemed to close in on her as her knees seemed to give away, filling her vision with black splotches. Faces blurred, and for the first time in her life she couldn't hear a thing. Then the world went black, and everything stopped.

***

"Get a wet towel for her head, please," Wren finally heard a sweet voice saying. She thought for a split second it was Valerie or Sammy, but when she opened her eyes just a crack, she found long raven hair connected to a more unfamiliar face.

"Wren?" the voice asked, bringing her closer back to earth. "You okay, sweetie?"

Something icy cold laid across her forehead and dripped into her hair. Wren's eyes began to separate figures from light as she finally saw Layla, the friendly detective—no, floater—who she had met earlier. Layla pushed an open bottle of water into Wren's hands and guided it to her mouth.

"Don't worry. I've got you," she cooed, eventually telling the crowd around Wren's body to disperse. "Take it easy. Here, eat this." She passed a cookie into Wren's fingers.

Wren broke a bit off and put it into her mouth. Her eyes were fully focused, and her senses slowly started to come back as the sugar hit her system. She felt the cold tile against her back, and when she realized what had happened she sat up with a jolt.

"Careful! Don't get up so fast!!"

"Did I pass out?" Wren gasped, lightly choking on the cookie.

"Yeah. Don't worry, it happens to everyone. Did you have anything to eat today?" Layla questioned, pulling Wren up from the floor and pushing her into a chair.

Wren thought back to her day. Everything was an emotionless blur. She couldn't remember eating a thing in the last thirty-six hours. She shook her head "no," her hair falling into her face, messing it up even more.

"Finish that cookie and I'll go get you a juice from the vending machine—" Layla started, getting up.

"No, wait! I can come with. I'm okay." Wren shoved the rest of the cookie into her mouth and smiled. "Really. I can come."

Though she obliged at first, a persistent Wren ended up following Layla down a dimly lit hallway. Each step she took she felt like she could breathe easier. The cookie made her feel much better as she awakened more with every breath, and she didn't like the idea of sitting alone in the waiting room. She trusted Layla. Her kindness was the only thing that kept Wren from completely falling apart when she was brought in.

"You scared the shit out of us." Layla chuckled, pushing a few quarters into the vending machine.

"Sorry."

"Seems like something in this precinct doesn't agree with you."

"What do you mean?"

"Last time you were here you puked all over Officer Rainer's trash can. Remember?"

"Oh, right..." Wren had forgotten all about that. She didn't want to make it seem like it was all a ruse. A sliver of fear crept in. "Do you think that looks suspicious?"

Layla was digging a bottle of cranberry juice out from the bottom of the vending machine. "What do you mean?"

"Like, does it look like I cause some scene whenever I'm in here? Like I'm trying to avoid those detectives by disrupting the office?" Wren's mind was tumbling through a million thoughts. This was exactly what she was trying to avoid during the investigation. She didn't need to draw more attention to herself.

"Well, the body has an involuntary response to things that make us uncomfortable, or scared, or even excited. Some might think you have something to hide..."

"Jesus Christ..."

"...and others will see it for what it is. You're a teenage girl who just lost a classmate. They just dragged you out of class in the middle of the school day. You're scared. That doesn't make you guilty—it makes you human," she reassured Wren, twisting off the juice cap and handing it to her.

"You're pretty biased for a detective." Wren cracked a smile.

Layla snorted. "Right... *a detective.* You have to be the only person around here who actually calls me that."

"What's the deal with that? I get there's some hierarchy, but they're not even letting you do your job?"

"You wanna know the real reason?"

Wren nodded her head, eager for something to distract her from her world burning down all around her.

"Because I go with my gut and it freaks them out. Everyone always says that they go with their gut, but they have mountains of evidence to back them up. But me? I just kind of know."

"And what do you know about Stella's case?"

"I know that you didn't do it. You and Stella didn't get along, but that doesn't really give you enough motive. I mean, did she even get along with anybody? I know that it was hard for me to even be around her."

Wren's ears perked up at that. "Wait, how did you know Stella?"

Layla froze for a minute, the realization of what she let slip finally hitting her. Before even thinking, she grabbed Wren's wrist and pulled her behind the vending machines, out of sight. "You can't tell anyone. This is the biggest case this precinct has seen in a while. I already don't exist here. If they find out that I knew her, they'll just find another excuse to throw me out."

"Layla, slow down! What are you talking about? How did you know Stella?" Wren's heart was hammering outside of her chest. She didn't think Stella would have any reason to know a cop.

"I ran into her on one of my breaks. I was just stepping out to get coffee and I found her crying and all alone on a bench, so I approached her. She was just really stressed about college, and that's why she was kinda falling apart. She didn't think she would get into an Ivy."

"She didn't."

"Well, I tried to calm her down a bit. I told her that I knew someone really high up at Dartmouth who might be able to help her. I met with her a few times to prep her for her meeting, but that was all."

"Why would she trust you? She didn't even really know you. Why would she just talk to a random cop about all this stuff?" Wren grilled Layla, still not entirely buying it.

"I honestly don't know. Maybe she didn't have anyone else to talk to about it. She needed some sort of connection to get into an Ivy, and I guess she was just hoping I could help her. I thought I could."

"Your connection didn't work," Wren realized, putting the pieces together.

"Unfortunately, no. I was just hoping I could help her, but I failed." Layla reflected. "The thing is, when you don't have anyone else to talk to, sometimes you put your trust in people who you don't entirely know and hope for the best."

Wren nodded, taking Layla's dismay as a true confession. She was just a person who wanted to help. It became clear to Wren that was all Layla ever did.

***

"No more fainting stunts. Alright, sweetheart?" Detective Moore smiled smugly.

"Detective!" Donovan hissed under her breath. "Are you okay, Wren? Feeling better?"

"Yeah. Layla got me a cookie and juice." Wren breathed a sigh, preparing for whatever bomb they were about to drop on her.

Donovan was seated at the table while Moore was pacing back and forth, making the room seem to shrink with every step.

"Why did you pull me out of class?" Wren questioned, eager to get to the point.

"We made a new discovery in the case. Forensics swept the scene, and while we thought the rain that day had washed away all vital evidence, it didn't. Our team found a blood stain that doesn't belong to Stella. The person whose blood this is could be the killer."

A pang of fear krept up Wren's spine. She knew exactly what it was. Wren's fingers traced her leg down to the scab on her knee from when she fell down that night. It was a little banged up and bled a little, but she would survive. She didn't think it could possibly get her into this much trouble.

"We would like to test your blood to see if it's a match."

Chapter 19

———

"They can't just do that!" Sammy gasped as Wren was retelling the story.

The whole crew came to Wren's house while her parents were still waist deep in paperwork from their office. She sent out an emergency text to her friends, and as if they had nothing else to do, they all showed up within minutes. Rohit would have done the same, if only he had decided to still be Wren's friend. If only he decided to still care.

"So what, now they have a sample of your DNA?" Tyler asked, nervously. He had been the first person to show up at Wren's house and gave her a huge hug when he saw her. When she had asked why, he simply responded by saying, "You looked like you really needed one. It's not bad to admit it. It doesn't make you weak." It was almost like he read Wren's mind.

Wren replayed the conversation from the precinct. She was still fuzzy after fainting, but alive nevertheless. She didn't know if the real reward was dying, but her punishment was to live through this purgatory called "life." She would live another day to battle out these

There are two sides to everyone...

misconceptions and fight for herself. "They don't have my DNA. They didn't have a warrant, so until they do, they're not getting anything from me," Wren stated with a slight shake in her voice.

"But will they get a warrant?"

"Probably," Mia bluntly stated. Everyone stopped and glared at her blunt honesty. "What? It's true. On high profile cases, they rush to get warrants. Especially in this town. How often does a murder investigation happen?"

"Okay, but you didn't have to say it like that. Be a little sensitive to the situation," Tyler muttered.

"No, Mia's right." Wren announced. "It'll be any day now, which is why we need to act fast." A mix of confusion fixated on everyone's faces. "Once they find out it's my blood at the crime scene, shit is gonna get a lot worse," Wren confessed, eager to get to work.

"But they're the police. There isn't enough evidence to prove it's you. And you didn't do it! They'll let you go," Derek explained, hoping that things would simply work itself out.

"My parents once told me something about the law. 'The truth doesn't matter when you find a piece that fits.' They aren't looking for who did it—they're looking for someone to blame." The words left Wren's mouth like a death sentence. They tasted bitter on her lips and hit her stomach with a pang of pain. The weight on her shoulders seemed to double, and all Wren could do was sigh and endure it until the end.

"You have a target on your back. Don't you?" Sammy asked, already knowing the answer.

Wren's chin fell to her chest as she took a deep breath. "Yes."

"Then we better get to work," Asa announced.

Everyone split up to find as much information as they could. Valerie set off to deliver her condolences and get some intel from Stella's parents; Mia and Derek went to talk to more people around school; Sammy and Tyler left to try and retrace places Stella frequently visited. Asa hung back to find a digital trace of things Stella did to see if there was any evidence of a stalker or a killer in her midst. Wren ventured into her attic in search of some supplies to lay out the evidence before her. As her fingers clasped around an old corkscrew board, a box fell, spilling fabric all over the floor.

She picked up the box only to drop it at the sight. Kids sized Halloween costumes littered the floor with lost memories. Rohit and her had always dressed up in theme. She found matching cowboy costumes and then eyed matching lab coats from the year they decided to go as mad scientists. She leapt to the floor, burying her face and arms in the small clothing, clinging to something that was long gone. She smelled the cheap polyester and found candy wrappers stuffed in pockets, longing to go back to those simpler times.

This was her childhood. Had she really wanted to change it that badly? Were things really even that bad before? She smelled the crisp fall air muzzled in the layers, as if she could be transported back in time when things were easier. Back when she would be able to change her mind and be okay with everything. And Rohit would still be there by her side. But Asa might not. And Derek, Valerie, Sammy, Tyler, and even Mia.

She might not have even known *herself* if she hadn't learned to live.

"Wren? Did you find it?" Asa hollered from downstairs.

Wren scrambled to put the costumes back in the box and tucked it away in the corner, locking those memories away in the back of her mind. She grabbed the corkscrew board and pulled herself together. "Yeah, just found it. I'm coming down now."

Asa knew something was wrong the minute Wren descended the stairs. A deafening silence had filled the air as she pulled the board down with her. He wrapped his fingers around it and said "I got it. I'll put it up for us."

Wren was grateful to not be alone through this. Before, she didn't think she needed anyone but Rohit. It was like she had been breathing without air all this time. She didn't realize how badly she needed everything else until she got it.

They worked in silence as he helped her put up note-cards of places to start looking for evidence. Long strings of red thread tied important factors together, slowly lacing into an incomplete web. Much of the board was blank, staring at them.

"You know," Wren finally broke her silence, "I wasn't very nice to Stella on her last day alive."

Asa chuckled. "You guys were never nice to each other."

Wren let a smile slip. "I know. This is like Stella's last 'fuck you.' She'd be pleased to see how my life got turned upside down over her death. She'd be happy to know how much destruction she's left behind for me to deal with." And just like that, Wren burst into a hysterical fit of laughter.

Asa was taken aback by this surge of emotions. Wren spiraled, gasping for air the more she guffawed. She clenched her arms around her stomach, wincing with each breath she tried to draw in. Something clicked in Asa's head. He threw an arm around Wren's shoulders and drew her body close to his. She laughed into his shoulder until it turned to heavy quick breaths as he gripped her harder in the embrace. Her heart was hammering away against his steady beat.

He put a hand on her head and stroked her hair, hushing her. "It's okay, Wren. It'll be okay," he cooed, trying to mask his own nerves.

A million thoughts flickered through Wren's brain as she gasped for air. She had been raised to always have the answer. Wren studied everything, and when she didn't know something she made sure to spend more time exploring the topic in detail. For once, Wren was completely dumbfounded. She didn't know everything, and even worse, no one knew exactly what happened. The confusion was suffocating her, setting her lungs ablaze as her breath quickened, no signs of it slowing back down.

"*Breathe*, Wren. We're going to count, okay? From one hundred. Count with me," he whispered, just above Wren's panting. "One hundred, ninety-nine, ninety-eight..."

It wasn't until halfway through when Wren's heart stopped racing and slowly aligned itself with Asa's calm chest. He held her tight the whole time, keeping track of her pulse and breathing. It started getting easier to breathe the tighter he held her. She could feel how his air was big and full and calm. She learned to time hers with his, finally reaching a state of normalcy, catching herself in the moment she could think clearly again.

"Thanks," Wren whispered, standing up after some time.

"Has that happened before?" Asa questioned, concerned. He still had his hand wrapped in hers, worried that something else might happen.

"No... it hasn't." Wren let her hand fall from his.

"Well, should we tell someone?"

"No..."

"Should I call your mom?"

"No!" Wren half shouted, desperate to forget about what just happened.

"Wren, you just had a panic atta—"

"I know, Asa!" Wren yelled before falling on the couch. "Can we just forget about it?" Wren buried her face in her hands, wishing everything would just stop.

Asa met her on the couch, carefully placing a hand on her leg, bringing her back to earth. His touch had that effect on people. "It's nothing to be ashamed of, Wren. You're under a lot of pressure. We all are."

Wren heaved a sigh and lifted her head from her palms. She couldn't bear to look him in the eyes. She hated how vulnerable she felt lately, but for the most part she was able to keep it under control. She was able to keep it contained. She was able to release when she was alone on the bathroom floor, clinging to the razor in hand. Now, it seemed like that wouldn't solve anything. It would just leave her more broken than before.

"I'm not perfect." Wren sighed, regretting the moment those words escaped her lips.

"So?" Asa replied, unphased.

Something shook inside of Wren's chest. He didn't care. Somehow, she found herself searching for his warm chocolate eyes. Her face filled with warmth as he placed a hand on her cheek, drawing her to him. He tasted her lips tenderly, as if he couldn't get enough of her.

"I don't care, Wren. No one is perfect. You do so much. Just let that be enough."

There was so much warmth in his words. She had felt a comfort that was a complete stranger until then. How he had the ability to make her heart skip a beat and feel comfortable in her own skin was such a mystery. But perhaps that was an answer she was okay with not knowing. Perhaps that was the *only* answer she was okay with not knowing. She leaned in again and pushed her lips against his in a *thank you*. They were tender and warm and pushed and pulled her in mesmerizing ways. She felt completely undone as he pulled her onto him. He had a hand on each side, gripping her thighs. She felt electric—and alive. It was the first time she felt okay since their night out. His hands traveled to her waist, exploring under the hem of her shirt. She could have kissed him for an eternity, his hands all she would need for the rest of her life, but he pulled away suddenly.

"Wren, I love this, and I love that you're feeling better, but we really need to get back to work." Asa exhaled, still desperate to taste her lips again.

There are two sides to everyone...

Wren felt her head nod. She kissed him one last time as he lifted her up, standing and placing her feet softly back on the ground.

"There's so much we didn't know about Stella." Wren sighed, staring at the unfinished evidence board.

"I know, but thinking about what we don't know isn't going to get us anywhere. Let's try to tap into her head. What was important to her?" Asa pointed out.

"School," Wren stated without having to even think about it.

Asa wrote school and college on notecards and pinned them up. "I remember that she was still working to get into an Ivy."

"Yeah. She hated that she was going to University of Michigan, no matter how hard she tried to make it sound like it was her choice."

"She never really struck me as the type to give up," Asa remarked, jotting down "University of Michigan" onto a card.

"She wasn't." And then something fit into place like a puzzle piece in Wren's head. "She would do anything to get ahead." Wren took the marker from Asa's hand and wrote a name down on a notecard. It was a small lead, but it was the only one she had. There was one person who knew Stella and was trying to help her get into an Ivy League school. The one who was scared for anyone to find out that she had a relationship with the deceased. Wren didn't want to believe it, but she had no other leads.

Wren pinned the card up on the board, tying a red string connecting it to Stella and college note cards. It read the name "Detective Layla Nazari."

Chapter 20

Layla Nazari was toying with the idea of putting herself out there.

Every day after work, Layla would be deliriously exhausted from her mundane workload, her snappy coworkers, and people in general. The part of her that wanted to be accepted into the work life culture decided to put her insecurities behind her and go to Dale's Pub, the local bar her precinct often went to.

Mornings would often consist of recalling the events at the bar the night before. Who challenged who to a game of darts? Who spilled beer all over themselves? Did someone go home with another officer? It was always filled with juicy gossip... gossip Layla was never a part of because she felt horribly unwelcomed.

She had decided that there was nothing wrong with going there to simply get a drink. Their precinct didn't own the pub, and it wasn't like these outings were invite-only. She planned to simply sit at the bar with a book in hand. At least it would be different from her day-in and day-out meals on her couch alone at home.

She figured that no one would notice if she went. It's not like they noticed her much at the precinct, but the second she pushed open the dark pub doors in the dimly lit room, she heard a chuckle and then a shout from the corner. "Layla! Here to take my coffee order?" It was Moore, raising a half empty glass of beer, slamming his arm down on the table like a barbarian laughing at a joke that wasn't all that funny or creative. The men around him joined in, guffawing at their pal's dry joke as if it were something taken straight from *SNL*.

Layla merely rolled her eyes, not allowing the laughter to hurt her even more. As planned, she made her way over to a stool at the bar and shrugged off her blazer, placing it on the chair next to her before taking a seat. She caught the bartender's eye. He was about six feet, tan skin, with a muscular build and tattooed sleeves crawling from his arms down to his fingers. He was polishing glasses off to his left when he saw Layla pull a book out from her bag.

"Dry martini. With an olive, please," Layla told the bartender.

He nodded and began mixing gin with a light drizzle of vermouth and garnishing with an olive. "How come I haven't seen you here before?" he asked, placing the V-shaped glass in front of her.

She looked up from her book, surprised someone was even talking to her as if what she said mattered. She shrugged her shoulders and took a sip of her martini. "I never come here."

"But you're a cop."

Her eyes raised. "How did you know that?"

"It's kind of hard to ignore their jokes from the back." He motioned to the table where Moore and his chums were, horribly manspreading, practically taking up three tables for only five of them. "I don't get it. What was so funny?"

"They don't take me seriously, so they give me all the shitty cases. It's their superiority complex." Layla shrugged.

"That's ridiculous."

Layla snorted while she took a sip. "Tell me about it."

"I'm Ethan." He stuck out his hand across the table.

"Layla." She took it with a smile forming in the corner of her lips. She was pleasantly surprised with his kindness. "So, are these guys a pain in the ass to serve?" she asked, nodding her head back to where her drunken team was.

Ethan chuckled, cracking his fingers nervously. "Sometimes, but they tip extra well when they're drunk. Sometimes they talk a bit too loudly about their cases."

Layla raised her eyebrows, concerned for the integrity of her team.

"Relax. I'm a bartender. My job is to just listen to people. I don't go around telling these stories," he explained, his hands in the air like it was a surrender.

"Well, it's always a shock when you hear that your coworkers are sharing case theories. Especially now." Layla's face dipped.

"With that girl, right? It's all over the local news. And he came in talking about how he was going to crack the case." Ethan nodded his head back Moore's way.

"Ugh, he's such an asshole. He's got it all wrong." Layla scoffed, taking another sip, letting the gin and vermouth dance on her tongue.

"How can you be so sure?" he asked, opening a beer for someone at the opposite end of the bar.

"I just am," Layla stated boldly, biting into her olive.

Her eyes analyzed him, the mysterious man on the opposite side of the bar. She liked the way his tattoos seemed to cover every inch of his upper body, even creeping up from the neck of his T-shirt. A part of her wanted to see what was underneath, if it told a story or if it was just for show. She took another sip from her drink, finishing off the last of the refreshing bitter taste.

"How about another one? On me," Ethan offered.

Layla tucked a lock of hair behind her ear and nodded, letting the warmth of the gin go to her cheeks. She bit her lip, watching him stir together a new drink. "What time do you get off work?" she asked him, savoring every bit of boldness that the drink was giving her.

He tried to hide a smile. "Nine." He added an extra olive into her new glass.

"What would you say if I asked for you to come back to my place after?"

He blushed. "I would say that sounds good." He tried to play it off cool.

"We can do all kinds of fun things," she whispered to him. "And you can tell me all about the other stuff my coworkers have been letting slip." She batted her eyelashes before taking a sip of her second drink.

He looked at her like he wanted to tear her clothes off then and there. All he could manage to do is nod his head, excited to really get to know her.

Chapter 21

———

Wren's head was reeling through the night. She had wanted to drive straight to the precinct and confront Layla about everything. She wanted to end it all, but Wren's parents advised her to not go near the police station.

Wren's father even insisted on driving her to school, as he didn't want Wren to follow her own agenda. "Honey, you're doing great so far. I know it's scary, but you have to lay low. We don't need to draw more attention to you."

Wren let the words float through her mind and out her ears. Everything was foggy except for the thoughts inside her head. Her Adderall had taken effect that morning, emphasizing every single thought she had. She was so focused on getting to the bottom of the case that nothing else could dissuade her.

"Are you listening to me, honey?" her father asked, concerned.

"Yeah, Dad," Wren muttered, taking a headphone out from her ear.

"We just want you to be safe. I know your mother can be hard on you, but we want what's best for you. We're trying to figure all this out, so just bear with us." He explained, pulling into the school parking lot.

Wren wondered for a moment why they were so adamant about her keeping her head down. Were they really just concerned for her well-being, or did they wonder something else? Did her father suspect the unthinkable? "Do you think I did it?" Wren found herself asking, curious if one of the people she trusted most in the world could find her guilty of such a crime.

Her father sighed, taking his glasses off and rubbing his eyes. "It doesn't matter what I think. It matters what I can prove."

Every hair on Wren's body stood up. Her stomach turned even more, now filled with the taste of bitter truth. She wondered if she would ever wake up not feeling this way again. "But do you think that, considering everything those detectives know, I could have done it?"

A piece of her father's heart cracked, hearing the worry in his sweet daughter's voice. She was always so confident and bold, even when she was scared, but he had caught the tiniest of tremors in her words. He pulled her close to his chest and breathed into her soft lavender hair. He could often see himself in his daughter, and that made him excited and scared. "Listen to me, honey. I know you didn't do it. Let's just hope that's enough for now." He kissed her on the forehead before unlocking the car doors and watching her climb up the school stairs to meet her friends.

There are two sides to everyone...

Wren knew she would be all the school would be talking about. Being pulled out of class by a police officer was a Richmond High first. She would be talked about for years to come. *Did you hear about that crazy smart girl who killed her classmate?* She could hear the rumored future stories with each step she took. Valerie and Asa had met her outside to walk in together, and Sammy, Derek, and Tyler were waiting by her locker.

"I appreciate all you guys are doing for me, but please," Wren heaved a sigh, "you're smothering me. I'll be fine on my own."

"We just didn't want you to be alone," Tyler explained.

"Yeah, these bitches smoking in the bathroom are already spreading rumors about yesterday." Mia scoffed.

"We've got your back." Derek smiled.

Something warm filled Wren's chest and she was miraculously able to take a break from the weight on her shoulders. She stopped fidgeting with her jammed locker and turned to fully look at the group. "I don't deserve you guys. You're all so loyal even with everything going on," Wren reflected, admiring how she had lucked out with finding such amazing friends so late in high school.

"We just don't want you to go through it alone," Valerie added.

"Yeah, we were all there that night. It only seems fair that we stick together. You're one of us now, Wren," Sammy promised.

"Thanks, you guys. Really. But right now, I just have to get through the day as normal as possible. I'll be able to survive it without you all crowding me. Seriously.

Go," Wren explained, adding a smile to nudge them on their way.

They dispersed begrudgingly, but Asa hung around. "So, about Detective Nazari... do you want me to go and talk to her if your parents—"

"No, I want to do it. Thank you, but I seriously don't think she'll talk to anyone else. She likes me. I need to confront her myself," Wren explained, pulling open her locker with a *clank*.

Dozens of scraps of paper came pouring out, each etched with something written on them. Asa bent down to help Wren gather them up when they both realized exactly what they said.

Killer killer killer

Confess

You killed her

Killer killer killer

Poor Stella

How do you live with yourself?

Killer killer killer

Rot in hell

Confess

All the air seemed to evaporate from Wren's body. She felt her fingers scramble to pick up every scrap and shove them into her backpack. Asa gripped her hand tight and whispered, "Throw them out right now."

Wren shook her head vigorously. "I don't want them falling into someone else's hands. It's going to look much worse if someone else finds it."

They rose from the ground, trying best to act nonchalant.

"I can't believe someone would do that to you. What kind of person would do that? Do you think it was Layla?" Asa asked, holding Wren closer to him so no one would hear.

Wren's eyes were darting from lockers to classrooms. She was eyeing everyone in the hallway, classmates, teachers, and all. "Or it was someone else. Just to mess with me. To scare me into having a meltdown or something."

"That's fucked up."

"So is my life." Wren groaned sourly.

"Hey," Asa started, pulling her toward him. He brushed his lips against hers briefly. "No it's not. We'll figure this out. I promise."

She smiled at his tenderness and how his warm hands felt against her clammy and shaky fingertips. "I hope so."

Wren set off to first period with her headphones in her ears. She kept her head down and insisted on doing work, although her teachers told her it was okay if she wanted to be excused. Keeping busy was going to get her through the day. She ran through scenarios in her head a million times. She knew she was going to confront Layla later that day, but what she couldn't figure out yet was the motive.

Perhaps Layla hadn't told her the entire truth. Maybe her and Stella weren't all that friendly. But that didn't make any sense. Stella was an ass-kisser at the least. She would take any opportunity to get ahead, so without question, she would try her best to impress Layla. Not to mention that Layla had come off incredibly sweet and caring. Wren sensed Layla's kindness the second she met her that first day at the precinct. She was kind and gentle and seemed like she was horribly misunderstood there.

How could she do something like this? Was she really that psychotic to kill someone and pin the murder on an innocent? And over what? An argument? A misunderstanding?

It was clearly more than a misunderstanding. Stella suffered from a blow to the head and then had been stabbed multiple times. This was something big. Wren couldn't even imagine what sort of line Stella had crossed to deserve the fate that ended her existence.

These thoughts flicked through Wren's mind all the way to lunch. Wren thought about calling an Uber to take her to the precinct right away, but her eye caught someone running from the cafeteria. Wren recognized Sammy's long curly hair and sparkly bangles jingling off her wrists. She was running away from the roar of the cafeteria noise, rushing to the girls' bathroom. Something shifted inside Wren's stomach, uneasy. She knew why Sammy was going back to that bathroom. She had caught her there before.

Wren rushed after her, her footsteps falling feet behind Sammy's quick steps. By the time Wren had reached the bathroom, she had heard the aftermath. Uneven panting was coming from the handicapped stall at the end. The toilet flushed before Wren knocked twice, whispering Sammy's name into the door. Another flush sounded before a click of the latch allowed the door to creak open. A beautiful Sammy laid completely undone on the bathroom floor. Her gorgeous curls were frizzing, and her eyeliner smudged near the ends of her eyes. Her lipstick was completely wiped off, and she had chills running through her skin. Wren fell to her knees and threw an arm around Sammy.

"Are you okay, Sammy?" Wren asked, squeezing her tight.

She held Sammy there, gently stroking her hair as Sammy collected herself. The bathroom door creaked open, and many footsteps followed. Before Wren could even close the door of the cubicle, she was greeted by Tyler, Derek, Mia, Asa, and Valerie.

"Not a good time, guys." Wren moved to close the door when it got caught by Derek's hand.

"We thought you guys came in here because of something with the investigation. Sammy, what's wrong?" Derek asked, sitting down on the floor, rubbing a hand on her shoulder.

"Derek, give her some space. You guys shouldn't even be in here. It's the girls' room," Mia pointed out to him, Tyler, and Asa.

Valerie took a water bottle out of the side pocket of Asa's backpack and handed it to Sammy. "Here you go, babe." Then after some time, she asked, "Do you want us to leave?"

Something of meaning hung in the air. They had all already seen each other at one of the lowest points in their lives.

Getting questioned by the police was never something they wanted to be a part of. Now more than ever, it felt like they were tied together by something like integrity or loyalty. Now, they owed it to each other to be there for one another, in both moments of happiness and great despair.

Sammy downed the water and thought how easy it would be to shut everyone out. She wouldn't have to deal with the worried stares or the pity hugs. But something really changed that day her and Wren shared their flaws. It was a new kind of release that she had yet to feel every time she tied her hair up and knelt before the toilet bowl hoping to flush away some shard of emotion. "You guys can stay," she found herself saying, and just like that, they all started filing into the handicapped stall. It was barely big enough to fit all of them, but something about it made Sammy feel safe and closer to these people than she ever felt with anyone else.

"We're here for you, Sammy," Mia promised, breaking the silence.

"Take your time. Whenever you're ready to talk," Tyler explained, giving her hand a squeeze.

Sammy took a deep breath before releasing everything that she was holding inside of her. The corner of her eye looked at the toilet water, longing to choke out more, but also desperately wanting out of the cubicle walls that had turned into a sanctuary for her. *No more*, she promised herself. *It's okay to be afraid. Just release.* "I have an eating disorder." Something about hearing the words out loud sent chills up her spine. Wren squeezed her hand, letting her know it was all going to be okay. "It started out being about weight and my figure, but..." A teardrop had dripped down her cheek. "...now it's more than that. It's about a release. And today, I... I really needed that."

There are two sides to everyone...

Sammy had explained how some of her friends had made fun of her for hanging out with a new crowd. They asked her if she even wanted to stay in their group or be on her own. They told her that if she was seen with anyone other than her usual gang, she would be out of the group. They had put her in a place far beneath them, happy to see her twitch in discomfort.

"They don't deserve a friend like you." Valerie comforted her, wiping away Sammy's tears.

"Those bitches. They think they're all high and mighty? They act like a bunch of lunatics every time someone pulls a bottle of vodka out." Tyler scoffed, offended for Sammy.

"The worst part is... they don't even know who I am. I always kind of changed myself to fit their group. I don't even know if that's the stuff I like. I don't even know who I am... and that's what sucks. That's how I ended up here," Sammy explained, avoiding eye contact. "Leaving that group... it leaves me with myself, and I don't really know who that is."

Silence fell upon them. Something about being crammed in the bathroom together had shifted their relationship with each other.

"I have an idea," Valerie beamed.

"That perky attitude tells me that I'm gonna hate this." Mia rolled her eyes from the corner.

"Probably, but you're one of us now. You have to participate." Valerie grinned, eager to change the subject. "We all know each other, but we don't know the deep stuff. So, everyone go around and say something that has been on your mind." She turned to Sammy. "Like a *release.*"

Valerie's voice was like a hug. Her ideas always had the power to convince anyone of anything, and it was empowering. She talked about everything so sweetly, that it would make almost anyone feel instantly comfortable.

"I'll go first," Asa offered, happy to use himself as a distraction. "Everyone is so excited about college and the next chapter of their lives. It makes me feel like something inside of me is wrong. I'm not trying to sound like one of those guys that peaks in high school, but I don't want all this to end. I want late night drives and sneaking out with no consequences." He looked at Wren, who chuckled. "Given there are no murder investigations of course." Lighthearted laughter filled the cubicle, already lightening the mood. "It just feels like every day, my life is just passing me by. And I don't want to get caught up in the college bullshit. Things will be different then. I just sometimes wish I could hold on to how things are now."

"I like to take pictures," Mia announced all of a sudden. Everyone was shocked to see Mia eager to share, but it seemed like she was slowly taking down the wall she always had between people. "I've always loved the vintage feel of things. I'd never admit it now because it's a trend, but I like pictures. That's how I met my boyfriend actually. I was going to this one abandoned bridge to take photos of some street art in Philly, and he was there too just goofing around. So, I started to take some pictures of him, and they turned out really great. There's just something about photography that feels different for me. It's like the perspective of everything. Normally, I'm pretty closed off..."

"You don't say." Derek smirked.

"Shut up!" Mia laughed. And she really laughed, filling everyone with a warm explosion of trust. "Normally I'm pretty closed off and don't understand people, but with a camera, it's like I see everything clearly. I wish I were like that all the time. More pensive instead of ready to attack everyone who looks at me. But I suppose that everyone has two sides to them."

"Thanks for sharing, Mia. That's the whole reason why we're doing this... to get to know each other even better," Valerie explained, dusting some dirt off of her skirt. "My turn, I guess."

Everyone turned, shocked to see Valerie having something she needed to get off her chest, but then what Mia said had sunk in. There are two sides to everyone.

"Like Asa, I'm scared. Most people are moving to a different city or state, but I'm going to be in a completely different continent. It seemed like a good plan for a while, but I'm so, so scared about everything. I've wanted to move to London for so long, and now that it's becoming a reality, I don't know if that's what I want. It just feels weird to not have everything figured out." Valerie finished. A look of relief washed over her after unloading what's been on her mind. A tiny bit released when she first told Wren about it, but this was better. She had a group of misfits that made her feel more complete than whatever life she was living before.

"I'm gay," Tyler confessed.

Another silence washed over the cubicle. Eyes met each other with shrugged glances. It was all broken when Derek slapped a hand on Tyler's back. "That's great man. I'm happy for you."

A grin slowly stretched across Tyler's face. It was beautiful and sent warm waves through everyone's core.

"When did you know?" Sammy asked.

"I think since I was ten. But I wasn't sure until I met someone. And after him, everything felt easier. That's how I knew." He shrugged. "I was never planning on 'coming out.' I just never felt the need to announce it. This is me, you know? I was just going to wait until I dated someone, and I would introduce him as my boyfriend. I don't know why I announced it like that. I just wanted you guys to really know me. I don't know... it's not a big deal."

"It's always a big deal when you can start being yourself," Wren told him, giving his hand a squeeze.

He smiled and thanked her by pulling her into a tight hug. Soon enough, everyone started throwing their arms around each other in a big group hug. In that moment, it didn't matter what people thought. It mattered that they were themselves.

"So what's your deal, Derek?" Mia asked, trying to break up the group hug.

"Nothing. There's nothing I need to get off my chest," he replied coolly.

"Oh c'mon, babe. There has to be something. You can tell us as much or as little," Valerie pressed.

"I killed Stella," he announced with a death glare.

Fear shot up everyone's spines at the same time, each member of the group trying to comprehend what Derek had just dished before them.

"W-what?" Wren choked.

A smile cracked in his face as he burst into a fit of laughter. "You guys should have seen your faces! That was epic." He guffawed. He pointed at Asa and Wren, still catching his breath. "You two aren't as smart as you let on because I was with everyone else all night. Not to mention that I'm not a psychopathic killer." Derek smiled.

Despite the intensity of the situation, it felt good to start cracking jokes about the state of things. A level of lightheartedness was necessary, and Derek had gotten the ball rolling. Wren chuckled, although she tried to fight it, but she was soon joined by everyone else in a fit of laughter.

"Alright, buddy. You're not getting off that easy. Tell us something. For *real* this time," Valerie instructed.

"You caught me. Typical Derek move to avoid the situation. Um, well... I didn't want to tell anyone this, but I, umm... I got into art school," He muttered, playing with his phone.

Asa stole the phone from his hands. "That's amazing dude! Why are you trying to hide it? That's a huge accomplishment!"

"Because..." Derek started, taking the phone back, "I can't afford to go. And that sucks. It's just something I'm dealing with right now. I just didn't want to announce it because the situation is kind of embarrassing."

"I'm sorry, Derek. But you could apply for—" Valerie started.

"I appreciate it, Val. But I hear this sort of thing from guidance counselors and my mom. I'm really tired of this and don't want to talk about it. I'm just not ready yet," Derek muttered.

She nodded right before turning to Wren. "Your turn, babe."

Wren smiled, grateful to have the platform to announce the discovery that she had made the previous night. "I recently accepted the fact that I am not perfect. And I am learning that that is perfectly okay."

Chapter 22

———

Wren was pleased with how the rest of the afternoon went. She had friends, actual and genuine friends. Despite that, she caught herself sneaking peeks over at Rohit from time to time, and sometimes she would catch him looking at her too, but in the end he wasn't going to be there for her. She hated how she had to think about it every day. She hated that he had that much control over her emotions. But more than anything, she hated that she just couldn't bring herself to let him go.

Asa had promised to drive Wren home that day. They were going to go into town and come up with a game plan on how to get Wren out of the prime suspect spot.

Asa was sweet. He waited for her after class and opened her car door when she got in. He did his best to make a difficult time better. She kissed him again and again. She wanted his lips on her all the time.

They had pulled into a parking spot right outside of the local coffee shop. Asa had gone in to order two large, iced coffees with a little bit of creamer. He figured that he would treat her after having a rough past couple of days. Wren was just about to let the happy music of Asa's playlist distract her when someone from across the street caught her eye. She recognized a figure with dark raven hair stepping out of the flower shop, juggling a coffee and her purse in hand. Before thinking twice, Wren jumped out of her seat and slammed the car door, marching straight toward Detective Layla Nazari.

"Wren! How are you doing?" she asked with a concerned head tilt.

Wren inched closer to Layla, trying to calm her voice before saying, "I need to talk to you. *Now.*" Wren nodded her head toward the hidden alleyway behind them, beckoning for Layla to follow her.

"What's up?" Layla asked, eyes widening, sensing the level of urgency.

"*What's up*? That's all you have to say to me?" Wren roared, every vein in her body pulsating with anger and betrayal and everything in between.

"Wren, I need you to calm down. *Please,*" she insisted curtly.

Wren took a deep breath, trying to settle her fury and accuse her with a clear and focused mind. "You haven't been honest with me about Stella."

Shame traveled up every inch of Layla's skin and made the hairs on the back of her neck stick up. She couldn't decide if it was those words that shook her to the core or that somebody had found out about her. "I don't know what you're talking about."

"Yes, you do. You said you were helping Stella try to get into Dartmouth, but you said you only met a couple

There are two sides to everyone...

times. That's not true, is it?" Wren challenged, every cell in her body filling with fire.

"No, it's not true," Layla blurted, just barely above a whisper.

"You saw her that night. The night she died..." Wren gasped. She wanted to believe it was someone else, someone less kind and gentle, but her suspicions were proving to be true.

"Yes." Layla breathed. "But it's not what you think."

Wren's mind was moving faster than the words that were tumbling out of her mouth. "Was she blackmailing you? That's the only thing that makes any sense. You told me about how the other cops didn't like you. Is there something you've been hiding this whole time and she figured it out, so you killed her? And you were just going to let me take the fall for it? Trying to get me to confess over something that I didn't do?" Wren demanded, trying to slow the millions of questions she had.

"I didn't kill Stella!" Layla pleaded.

"Yeah, right."

"I have an alibi. I was at the precinct working the night shift at the time. But I did see her that day," she explained, setting down the flowers she bought on the ground. "I didn't say anything because of the investigation... and I felt guilty."

"Guilty?" Wren's mind was reeling. Her brain was foggy and hyper focused at the same time that she felt like she was going to explode.

"Yes. That was the night I met with her to explain that my connections at Dartmouth didn't work out. She wasn't going to get in, even after all that work. I tried my best to put in a good word for her, but it wasn't enough. She wasn't really happy to hear that. We argued and she stormed out. I didn't see her again."

"So why do you feel guilty? It's not your fault that she didn't get in," Wren pointed out, still skeptical.

"Because of our ugly argument. It was really horrible. I tried to be consoling, but she came at me as if it were all my fault. I was helping her out as a favor, but she saw it as her ticket in. I guess reality hit. It was probably one of the worst arguments I've ever had. I feel like I should have handled things more maturely, but—"

"Stella could make the most civil people manic."

"Yes. And I felt like maybe our argument led to the events that got her killed. Maybe she got herself into a dangerous situation and it was because she felt so angry with me. That's why I got these flowers," she explained, picking them back up. "I was going to drop them off at her parent's house to offer my condolences," Layla confessed.

For the first time, Wren saw what really got her to trust Layla the first time she met her. Layla cared. Heat rushed to Wren's face, making her feel ridiculous for coming at Layla with such fury. She was just scared, like Wren.

"I'm sorry, Layla."

"It's okay. I get it. You're just trying to figure everything out."

"No offense, but I really wanted it to be you," Wren found herself saying. "It would put an end to all this, and

I could breathe again. I wouldn't have to worry about being followed or getting tormented at school."

"Wait, you're being followed?" Layla questioned, her eyes widening.

"Only once or twice. It's some black truck. But today I got some threatening notes in my locker."

"Give me the notes," Layla commanded with her hands out.

Wren opened her backpack and pulled a handful of scraps of paper out. She watched Layla flick through them, analyzing them as if they were a part of some massive puzzle.

"Is it okay if I take these back to the precinct? I'm going to try to compare them to any other forms of paperwork we had people sign. Maybe I can find who did this and we might get a better lead."

"You'd do that for me?" Wren asked, feeling her eyes tear up.

"Of course, sweetie! It helps to have a friend who's a cop. I'm going to try to figure this out."

"Thank you." Wren felt something close to relief ease her mind.

"But I need to protect my job too. I want to tell you something, but you didn't hear it from me. You have to swear that you won't tell the other detectives," Layla whispered as people walked by.

"Okay, I promise."

"I did some digging and I found out that Detective Moore thinks your prescription of Adderall mixed with the alcohol you had that night may have caused some form of a hallucination. It's rare, but it happens from time to time. Because of the rain that night, it's still hard to narrow down the exact time of death, so they think it's possible that after you went home that night, you came back out and—"

"Killed her? You know how insane that sounds?" Wren shrieked.

"I know it sounds insane, but that's the strongest lead they have. And if that blood is going to be a match..."

"It will be a match." Wren gasped, panicked.

"Huh?"

"I fell that night and scraped my knee. I was bleeding. It's my blood."

"Shit, Wren. We need to figure this out as soon as possible," Layla stated, neatly placing the notes in a Ziploc bag from her purse.

"I know."

"Lay low for a while. If you find something, you text me. I'm going to do everything I can to help you," she promised, typing her number into Wren's phone.

"Thank you."

Wren left feeling much worse than she had when the whole investigation started. She *had* to hope that Layla would come through on her promise to help her.

If the cops didn't get to her first.

Chapter 23

Asa and the rest of the gang joined Wren at Sundae's Ice Cream Shop to go over everything they've been on the lookout for. To their dismay, there was nothing out of the ordinary during their deep dive into Stella's life. Stella was a good student with good grades and a good life. Other than getting mad at a couple Starbucks baristas for getting her order wrong, no one had a dying urge to kill her.

Wren was beginning to see why she was the prime suspect.

It was just about the only thing that made sense.

"Detective Nazari is on our side, Wren. She'll figure something out," Sammy offered, hoping to bring some light to the situation.

"Unless the other asshat detectives get to her first," Mia pointed out.

"Thank you for that positive outlook, Mia." Derek scoffed, sarcastically.

"Maybe we should all go home. Your parents will be mad if we're hanging out too long." Wren was worried, ready to crawl into a ball and call it quits. She didn't want them to see her surrender to the accusations. She was exhausted from putting up a brave front.

They slowly filed out, all promising to help Wren no matter what. She wished their promises would be enough to get her out of this predicament.

Wren drove home, checking her rear-view mirror over and over again just in case the black truck was following her, but that night the roads were fairly empty. Paranoia crept in through her lungs, but what was she going to do about it? There were no solutions, and every answer seemed so far out of reach. She felt defeated and was planning to skip dinner entirely, crawl into her bed, and let her brain rot away to the endless episodes Netflix contained when she got a text as she pulled into her driveway.

Ria: come over now? home alone and miss you

Wren didn't know what to think. Did Rohit's little sister want to apologize for everything going on? Did she have a message to pass along? Wren was about to text her back, declining, but before she knew it she was out the door and already walking in the direction of the Kumar house. Her legs were bursting with new energy, like they themselves needed answers, companionship, and to feel welcomed again in a house that used to be like her second home.

An eager Ria jumped into Wren's arms the minute she opened the door. Ria had always idolized Wren. She looked up to Wren more than her brother, and the time without her had been brutal. Anytime Wren was over to hang out with Rohit, she would be sure to drop in and spend quality time with Ria. They had a bond that was special. In a different world, they would be really close sisters.

"I missed you, Wren!" Ria exclaimed into Wren's shoulder, still squeezing her into an embrace.

"I missed you too, Ria," Wren found herself saying.

"I'm so sorry about everything that went down between you and my idiot brother." She sighed, letting go.

"He did what he had to do."

"No, he's a coward. Friends don't leave friends behind when they need help," Ria ranted, leading Wren up to her room. It was like Ria had forgotten about her mother banning her and Rohit from hanging out with Wren. It was like old times again.

Wren had missed the way the Kumar house smelled. Spices and herbs filled the air and made everything feel warm. She missed the way the orange painted walls and traditional Indian artwork transported their visitors to an Indian getaway. The whole house was tied together through vibrant colors, making it look like an actual home instead of her own boring house.

"Where is everybody?" Wren asked, not sure if she wanted to catch Rohit in his room or if she never wanted to see him again.

"They went to the precinct to answer more questions or something." Ria shrugged, nonchalant.

"Oh..." Wren didn't know what to say next, but something in her decided to ask, "Do they hate me?" She hated herself for asking that. It made her look pathetic and weak, but Ria looked up to her too much to even think that.

"Wren, I don't think anyone could hate you. It's not possible. This is just a rough patch and they're all scared, so they just need some space."

"But not you?"

Ria smiled at that. "I always considered myself the black sheep of my family. I never agree with them, but my brother—"

"Always does. I know," Wren interjected.

"He made a big mistake, you know. I catch him pacing in his room all the time. Mom thinks he needs to pick up a new skill if he has that much time to pace."

Wren snorted at the thought of Mrs. Kumar catching Rohit wasting time by walking back and forth in his room. If he wasn't studying or adding new skills to his resume, he was wasting time. Well, he was never wasting time when he was hanging out with Wren. She was the exception. She was always welcome there. *Was.*

"How are you doing with all of this?" Wren asked.

"Well, I've been off the hook for a while. Indian parents love to focus on imperfections, and Rohit brought the motherload of disappointments in. So I'm kind of the golden child now." Ria laughed lightheartedly.

"Glad to hear that you're enjoying it. Staying out of trouble?"

"Always... you?" she asked, eyes filled with worry.

Wren sighed, ready to accept her fate. "It's not looking too good."

"I'm sorry. Is there anything I can do?"

Wren felt her cheeks grow warm. Of course Ria would want to offer to help with things that were out of her

There are two sides to everyone...

control. It was humbling and amusing, but suddenly Wren found herself in need of something Ria could do. "Distract me, please. Tell me anything going on in your life. I need a break from mine."

"You got it."

Ria told Wren all about how she really liked this one boy in her math class. She was nervous whenever she talked to him, and that reminded Wren of Asa. Ria went on to talk about how an end of the year bonfire was happening and she was hoping he would ask her to go with him. She asked Wren for advice on what to do. It felt good to be the one who people turned to and ask questions instead of this past week where she had all questions and no answers. It felt good to talk so casually with someone. For a while, Wren forgot about the investigation altogether. It was like things were normal again.

"I have to go to the bathroom. I'll be right back." Wren excused herself after the long conversation.

Wren took a turn down the long and familiar hallway. She was about to walk into the bathroom when she saw a light on in the corner room, Rohit's room. Without thinking, she was turning the doorknob and going into the room she spent so many days in. Everything was exactly the same, which for some reason pained Wren. Her best friend was changing so much, but his room had looked exactly how she remembered it. There were still stacks of books in every corner, a neatly kept desk, a well-made bed, and a small collection of photos speckled on his dark blue walls.

Wren traced her fingers from the carefully woven bed sheets all the way onto the desk. Stacks of books bordered the ends, one in particular, sticking out. All of the books had cracked bindings, and the pages were bent in at the corners, bookmarking pages that Rohit left off. This one book had barely been cracked open. There were no pages folded over, yet it was in the middle of the stack where Rohit put his recently read books. Like an itch she needed to scratch, Wren tugged on the book in the middle, sliding it out. She opened it only to find a scrap of paper inside of it. It was a note.

Stella—you look beautiful as always. Meet me after school.

———

There are two sides to everyone...

Chapter 24

Rohit didn't know what to expect when he got the urgent text from Wren. He was on his way home from the precinct when he got the message.

Wren: Meet me in the woods ASAP. We need to talk NOW.

He toyed with the idea of blowing her off, but he missed her. He hated how he was acting. He hated that these days, she was surrounded by new friends and he was just another face in the hallway. He wanted his best friend back, even if it meant facing the wrath of his immigrant parents who strictly forbade him to see her again.

When they got home, he waited anxiously in the kitchen until everyone went to their rooms. His parents would be on the phone talking to relatives in India, and since his night out, he was excluded from the conversations. There was nothing for Rohit to show off lately.

He left the garage door open and slipped out when it seemed like everyone else was preoccupied. He felt himself wishing that he changed his clothes or combed through his hair again. He wondered if the bags under his eyes showed how he stayed up late thinking about what he was doing and if any of it was worth it. His hands were shaking so much that he had to stuff them into his pockets. As he made his way through his backyard, he could make out a figure behind the silhouette of the trees. His stomach did backflips, and he chewed his lip to hide how nervously excited he was to see her.

"Wren." He breathed, placing a hand on her back.

She slapped him, fire filling his left cheek. He was completely caught off guard, but he should have expected something like that. She was always rougher with him, but she would never slap him like that normally.

"You asshole."

"I'm sorry, Wren," he pleaded, his hands searching for hers.

She snatched her hands away, something new in her face. It was more than exhaustion and the normal signs of stress in her eyes. It was something he had never seen in Wren before. She was scared.

"What the hell is this?" Wren demanded, shoving a paper into his hands.

Shivers went up Rohit's spine instantly. His hands shook as his fingertips grasped the edges. He didn't need to read it. He already knew what it said. He had read it a million times over and over again. "How did you get this?"

"That doesn't matter!" Wren deflected, angered by the betrayal.

"Answer the question, Wren! Did you go through my things?" His voice was growing angrier. He felt violated and shameful, like she had truly discovered him at his worst.

"Yes, I went through your things!" Wren shouted, irritated at his lack of focus. "Ria invited me over to talk and I went into your room. Now you better tell me, what the hell is this?" she growled, anger boiling through her veins.

"Wren, it's not what you think."

"What do you mean, it's not what I think? You wrote her this note. You were seeing her! And you hid it from me! I'm supposed to be your best friend," she yelled, clutching her hand to her chest as if he had reached in and ripped her heart out. "What the fuck is this? Did you hurt her?" Wren was practically screaming. She had to lower her voice for risk of falling apart entirely.

"You know I didn't. You know I would never hurt anyone." Rohit's chest burned at hearing all those accusations.

"I don't know what to believe anymore! I don't even know you!" Wren shouted, and this time, she couldn't hold back the tears.

"That note did belong to Stella, but I didn't write it. The last day she was in school, she dropped a bunch of stuff in the hallway," he explained, recalling the moment that played over in his mind so many times. The last time he talked to her before she died. It haunted him. "She was scrambling to pick up a bunch of these papers, so I went to help her. There were tons of these scraps of paper that came from her locker, but she wanted to keep them. So I helped her, and I guess one of her notes got mixed in with my stuff. And that's what that is."

"And you didn't report it? Ro, this is a solid lead. Someone else was involved in her life! Do you know that I am the prime suspect in this investigation? They've spun together this whole story that makes me look like a psychopath. Meanwhile, you've been sitting on something as big as this note!" Wren shouted, her throat aching and growing scratchy.

"I don't know why I didn't report it before. I was scared and my parents didn't want me to draw any attention to myself. They didn't want me to lose everything." Rohit tried to explain.

"But you were okay with *me* losing everything? Over something that I didn't even fucking do?"

"You know me, Wren."

"Do I? Because the Rohit I knew wouldn't abandon me when I needed him around. He wouldn't try to hide after we had the best night of our life—"

"That wasn't the best night of our life! Jesus Christ! Do you really believe that? That night made our whole lives shit!" he shouted back. Something fiery was pulsating throughout his body.

"You thought it was a good idea too!" she countered. "I signed up for a night out to be normal, not to be the prime suspect in a murder investigation!" Wren searched for air in her lungs but couldn't find it. She couldn't believe that her body would give up in her time of need.

"You did that to yourself, not me. You made me sign that fucking contract! You roped me into this mess. And *now* look what you've done! So much for having a casual night out!"

Wren felt the anger pulse in her veins. She felt that she was going to explode as her entire world began to burn around her. "You asshole! Are you not your own person? Why did you do it then? I didn't force you to! I didn't force your parents to sign on the dotted line! Why the fuck did you come with me?" Wren screamed.

"Because I love you!" Rohit screamed back.

And with that he wrapped a hand around her cheek and pulled her toward him. He kissed her angry lips, hoping that somewhere inside she would feel the same as him.

Wren did not kiss him back. She didn't move her arms, or head, or anything at all. She was too disgusted to even touch him. Her mind was on fire and her body was burning. How dare he have the audacity to kiss her? How could he do that? How could he think that was okay? In that moment she wanted nothing to do with her best friend, because he fucked up, not her, and she wasn't going to stand there and take the blame for him loving her. She wasn't going to do it. She was worthy of better.

Rohit let go and backed up, averting his eyes. It was like he knew he shouldn't have done it, but he couldn't go much longer harboring that secret. He thought this would explain some things to her. He thought it would explain why he was only crazy with her, why he was his best version of himself with her, but it only made him feel even more disgustingly vulnerable. Somehow, the silence loomed over them much worse than when they weren't talking. He looked at her again with longing desperation. Wanting to be taken back. Wanting to be with her.

"Oh god, please just say something," Rohit murmured.

"You don't get to do that," Wren choked, not meeting his eyes.

"Wren," he spoke softly, putting his hand around her fingers.

This only made her more infuriated. He had pointed the blame at her in both the eyes of the law and in their friendship, and now he had crossed so many lines. She pushed him hard, throwing him off balance for a second.

"Fuck you, Ro! You don't get to say you're in love with me and then kiss me like my feelings don't even matter! I don't love you."

"Wren, please—"

"If you loved me, you would want to protect me!" Wren screamed so violently, it nearly split him in two.

With nothing left for her there, she stormed off, realizing that she felt more lonely than she had ever felt in her whole life.

Chapter 25

——

"Bring her in," Detective Moore advised Detective Donovan. They were about to administer a blood test that would make a major break in their case.

Donovan fought the urge to put her partner in his place and simply complied. So much had happened since the investigation started. It was no surprise when the chief requested that Moore guide her in leading the case, since he always had more faith in men than in perfectly suitable women. Donovan opened the door to a frightened looking Wren Clements and her disgruntled mother.

"Have a seat. It'll be over before you know it." Moore smiled, smugly.

"Just a little bit of pressure on your arm, honey," Donovan explained, trying to make Wren comfortable given the circumstances. Unlike her partner, this brought her no joy.

"This is absolute bullshit," Wren's mother fired. "Wren told me she tripped that night, scraping her knee. Of course the blood will match."

"Frankly, ma'am, we just need to test the blood. If it's a match we'll go from there," Moore stated plainly, as if all of a sudden he was trying to hide the fact that he was excited to finally have someone pay for this crime.

The words echoed through Wren's ears as she slowly dissociated from what was happening. *Maybe I can think it away*, she hoped. Every movement was a blur. She couldn't remember what happened five seconds before. Everything just merely seemed to exist. It was like she was numb after everything that happened the night before. It had already been replayed in her mind too many times that it had seemed to lose all meaning.

"What happens now?" Wren asked, once a sample of blood was taken from her. Slowly, all the blood seemed to drain from her face. She bit into a cookie. Layla must have given it to her beforehand. She seemed to lose her sense of time as the countdown began until she was in handcuffs, no doubt arrested for probable cause.

"Now, we send it to the lab to see if it's a match. It'll only take a few minutes and then we'll know," Donovan explained, passing the vile to a young forensics specialist at the door.

Five minutes later, a knock sounded at the door. Wren and her mother jumped at the sound rapping on the metal, expecting the impending sentence. To their surprise, Layla appeared out of nowhere, purpose in her face and her heart on her sleeve.

"We don't need any coffee, Layla." Moore snorted.

"I'm not here to take your order. I'm here to talk to Detective Donovan actually," Layla announced, gaining more confidence in her voice toward the end.

Donovan would do anything to get out of time spent with her partner. The longer she spent with him, the more the days seemed to slow down and blend together as one dull week. She felt drained by his very presence, and so without asking any questions Donovan got up from her chair and met Layla in the hallway.

"What's up?"

"Wren didn't do it," Layla insisted.

"Your evidence?"

"I've been looking through security footage at their high school. Wren told me that someone was harassing her... leaving notes in her locker telling her to confess. It very well could have been some teen drama and someone trying to scare her, but something didn't feel right... So I did some digging and went through the security camera footage and while no one shoved anything into her locker during the day, I found something very interesting at around eleven the night before. Have a look for yourself." Layla passed her phone with the downloaded footage to Detective Donovan.

Donovan pushed the "play" button and watched the dark empty hallway. A large hooded figure came into the frame, hands filled with scraps of paper, keys jingling in their fingers. The figure unlocked the locker with ease, shoving the papers inside. Then, they closed it and scurried out of frame.

"Looks about six foot, and based on the build and the way that they walk... maybe middle aged male." Donovan locked eyes with Layla, stricken by the intensity of her realization. "We've been wrong this whole time. It isn't a teenager or a classmate who did it. It's someone older.

And based on how he knew where Wren's locker was and how to get in... He works at the school."

"You have to question all of the staff now." Layla nodded, nervous to open the can of worms waiting for them.

"No, *we* have to. Really good catch, Detective Nazari," Donovan complimented.

Layla's eyes widened with compassion. She felt as though she could hug Detective Donovan. "You called me Detective!" She grinned, giddy with delight.

"That's your title, isn't it?" She smiled. She never understood why people didn't treat Layla seriously. She was a good detective. That was just another reason Donovan hated working there. When the women were good at things, it scared the insecure men, and so they were sentenced to either ride the desk or be a secondary in investigations. God forbid they would ever step out of their place. But no more. "C'mon, let's go back in and brief Moore," she decided, opening the door.

Tumbling after her came a forensics specialist. He barged through the doors with such force, even Moore was thrown off for a second. "The blood doesn't match." He reported, winded from the urgency he fled the lab with.

"What?" Moore asked, utter surprise and a tone of disappointment in his voice.

"It's not a match. It's not Miss Clements."

Wren whipped her head around, unsure if it was some practical joke and they would still slap some handcuffs on her. She glanced at the specialist who stood with his hands on his knees, panting and shaking his head.

He looked at her and nodded, letting her know that the news was completely true. Her chest filled with relief and nerves, leaving her shocked at the turn of events. How could it not be her blood? She was confused and grateful all at once. It felt like a beautiful present or a streak of good luck or some sort of light at the end of this dark tunnel. Wren's mother even pulled her daughter to her chest and embraced her, as if it were normal. They both could get used to that feeling. The feeling of being on the brink of normalcy again.

"You're free to go now, Max," Moore dismissed the forensics specialist. "Well, well, looks like you got off easy this time—"

"This time? Seriously, Detective Moore?" Donovan asked, levels in her voice rising. "The blood doesn't match. She's done. She isn't a prime suspect in this investigation anymore."

Moore rose from his seat all of a sudden. "You mean *my* investigation."

"No, *my* investigation. It started out that way, but because you're a man and the captain thinks you're all high and mighty, you got to take the reins. And ever since then, we have gotten nowhere! You have dragged me in circles instead of actually looking for the person who did this. Detective Nazari has made a major discovery in the case. I would like to relieve you of your position and have her fill in." Donovan spoke as if nothing else mattered. In a way, nothing else did. She was tired of the sexism and people calling her "sweetheart." Women are a force to be reckoned with, and it was about damn time they got the credit they deserved.

"You can't do that. You need the captain's orders." Moore grinned in his usual condescending manner. "I'm sure he'd be happy to hear that you are undermining his wishes."

"I don't give a *fuck* about his wishes. I'm here to do what's right. C'mon, Detective Nazari. We have a murderer to find." She walked out, unafraid of any of the consequences she might have to face later.

"C'mon, Wren. You're free to go." Layla smiled, offering her hand to help Wren up from her chair.

Wren leapt up, seemingly floating off the ground. Her heart was palpitating. She didn't have that same sort of weight on her chest. She could overcome the nerves and stress she endured during the investigation and come out stronger than before. She could still live her life.

They found Detective Donovan in the parking lot lighting a cigarette. She was smiling to herself, giggling before taking a puff.

"I just wanted to thank you, Detective," Mrs. Clements said, shaking Donovan's free hand.

Donovan shook her head, still smiling. "Please, that was all Detective Nazari's work. She discovered security footage that led to a major discovery in the case."

"Thank you so much, Layla." Wren hugged her, finally feeling all of her tension release that was squeezing her together. She could breathe again.

"Of course. I told you, I always listen to my gut." Layla smiled, releasing Wren from the embrace. "That was badass, Detective Donovan. No offense, but I always thought you were a prude with the whole 'no cursing' thing."

Donovan took a long drag from her cigarette before stomping it out. "Claire. Please, call me Claire. And I don't usually, but he really fucking deserved it."

"He does," Wren piped up. "He made the rest of senior year a shitshow. And worse, he didn't even catch the killer." Wren sighed, still upset that a murderer was still walking free.

"I'm sorry about him. Cops like him look for what's convenient, not what's right. They're too lazy to do their jobs, but that's why Detective Nazari and I are here."

"Right. So, what's the new lead?" Wren asked, curious as to who could have possibly taken her spot as the prime suspect. Curious as to who hated Stella so much to kill her.

"Wren, that information is confidential. Let the detectives go on with their investigation." Her mother advised, already whipping out her car keys, ready to go home and never step foot in the precinct again.

"Actually, Mrs. Clements, I don't think we could have gotten this far without Wren's help. If she hadn't told me she was being targeted, we would have never found this." Layla showed Wren and her mother the screen capture of the dark figure before her locker. "We can't do it without her."

The gears were turning in Wren's mind. She was relieved, excited, worried, and riding a wave of adrenaline that made her hyper focused. "I'd be happy to help, but we're going to need to talk to a few more people." Wren grinned, excited to tell her friends the news.

***

"So you guys made your own evidence board," Detective Donovan pointed out, analyzing the different clusters on the board, impressed. There had been a few more notecards and red threads connecting ideas pinned to it since when they started, but it was still filled with dead ends.

"Yes. We wanted to do whatever we could to help Wren," Valerie explained, giving Wren's hand a squeeze. The gang was elated when they heard that Wren was no longer the prime suspect. Their first mission was complete.

"We had to try to figure out what it was like to be Stella. She was pretty private, so it was hard to figure out any sort of motive for someone to kill her," Tyler chimed in.

"You have nothing under the 'love life' category," Layla pointed out. "What? No partner of sorts?"

"No, god no." Mia scoffed.

"What Mia means is that Stella was always caught up in schoolwork and getting ahead of her peers. But things change..." Wren thought about telling them about the note in Rohit's book, but she resisted the urge. As much as he had hurt her, she wasn't willing to throw him under the bus in the same way he did to her. He could get in major trouble for withholding evidence. "Stella rejected everything that could possibly hold her back. If it didn't help her, she wasn't interested," Wren explained, memories of Stella playing through her mind like an old movie.

"So she did whatever she could to get ahead. Did she ever do anything crazy before? Anything out of the ordinary?" Donovan questioned, eager to get inside of Stella's head.

"There was one time..." Asa started to explain, locking eyes with Wren. She nodded in approval. "She started a rumor about Wren."

"Wren has ADHD, but Stella took it as an opportunity to tell people that Wren didn't actually need the Adderall and she only used it to look better in school. Everyone believed it and thought Wren was a big faker," Derek explained, taking over for Asa.

"Some people still do." Wren sighed. "It's hard to deny something like that when you actually need to take medication consistently."

"Was she happy about the rumor?" Donovan questioned, taking notes on a notepad.

"She liked causing destruction as long as it didn't affect her," Sammy replied coldly.

Amidst the discussion, Layla suddenly jumped out of her seat and stared at the evidence board before them. She ran her fingers through the papers, whispering things to herself. She was in some sort of trance, unaware of how many people were watching her. Then, she snatched a string and connected the card that said "love life" to "college."

"The kids said she didn't have a love life, Detective Nazari," Donovan pointed out, confused.

"That we know of… It's the only thing that's completely blank on here. Teenagers keep secrets all the time. What if this is it? What if the reason she kept it a secret is because she was using him to get into a better college? She would do anything to get ahead." Layla spiraled off, her inner thoughts spilling out into a confusing frenzy.

"But who could she possibly date who would help her get into an Ivy?" Sammy questioned, trying to think of anyone she knew who would do that.

"Someone who has access to things like grades and even college connections… maybe a teacher." Donovan breathed. She whipped out the footage that caught the man in question. "All of you, look at this. Do you recognize him?"

Everyone crowded around the phone, replaying the video over and over again to try and make out the dark figure.

"No, we can't see anything," Derek said with a tone of apology.

"Then we need a list of teachers that Stella had. We're going to find the son of a bitch who did this," Donovan declared, already searching through her laptop for shadowless faces.

Chapter 26

———

The next morning, Detectives Donovan and Nazari took their investigation to Richmond High. They wanted to go through the school unnoticed, only informing the principal of their search in order to not alert any of the faculty.

Like everything else in high school, word of their investigation caught on quick and travelled through the halls like rumors. Mostly it was from people who didn't have their facts straight. They all thought the detectives were looking for more evidence against Wren and the rest of her gang, and somehow it worked in the detectives' favor. No one was expecting the staff to get called in for questioning at first.

They tried to be discrete, making sure there wasn't enough time for the faculty to fabricate some story as their alibi. Their search for the culprit lasted the whole school day. They made their way through the directory, making sure to interview the male staff, trying to latch on to any sign of fury or numbness. It was hard trying to find some overarching behavior. Richmond High was a large school with a thousand kids per grade, and memories of old students sometimes blurred together. One thing they all knew was that Stella was intelligent and destined for great things, and it was a shame that her time was cut short.

The day was done almost as soon as it began. Although yesterday had felt like they were getting somewhere in the investigation, everything seemed to move in slow motion as the actual investigating was underway. No one raised any sort of red flags. This was just what they needed: a criminal right under their nose with no means of catching them. It was like the stench of failure was creeping into their clothes and hair, embodying every moment of their investigation.

Layla sat at a table in the empty cafeteria as the school emptied out the last of the students. She sifted through her stack of papers, each of which she had to get more background on the suspects. She had each of them print their names and sign at the end of the form. Her eyes glistened, analyzing the careful strokes of some signatures versus the jagged rushed angles of others.

"I'm gonna go grab a coffee from the teachers' lounge. Want one?" Claire Donovan yawned, exhausted with how inconclusive the investigation was going. High school clearly drained the life out of much more than its students.

"Yeah, thanks." Layla smiled dryly, still analyzing signatures in her stack of papers.

Someone lingered in the corner of her eye. She saw an Indian boy, about six feet tall, trying to figure out if he should stay or go home. She recognized his shyness when he wasn't around his other half. She remembered

There are two sides to everyone...

his overprotective mother and knew him instantly from the precinct.

"It's okay. I don't bite, Rohit." She winked, gesturing for him to come over.

He reluctantly trudged over, checking the corners to see if anyone was watching. The hallways were clear, all signs that everyone was home for the rest of the day. "You work for the police?"

"Lay—actually, Detective Nazari." She extended a hand to meet his. He took it and shook firmly. "Is there something on your mind?"

"If you're here for Wren again, she didn't do it," Rohit blurted out.

"I know she didn't. Your best friend is safe. We're looking for someone else, actually." She dangled the hint at her search to see if he knew anything at all. She was hitting a dead end and she wasn't ready to give up just yet.

He exhaled, relieved that Wren was going to be okay. He hadn't stopped thinking about her since he felt her lips on his. Since she told him that she didn't love him back. Rohit didn't want to be that guy anymore. He wanted to be his old self again, iced coffee in the park, long bike rides, and movie nights by her side. He thought about giving up entirely on himself, but Wren was right. He owed it to her to make things right again. No more being scared.

"I have something for you." He confessed, digging the paper out from his backpack. "I ran into Stella the last day she was alive. She dropped this note and it got mixed in with my stuff. I think it can help with the investigation." He passed it to Detective Nazari with a shaky hand. "I'm sorry I didn't turn it in sooner. I should have, but I was scared it would mess with graduation or college or... No, sorry that isn't a good excuse. I should have turned it in before. I'm so sorry."

Rohit waited for Layla to say something. He waited for her to yell at him and tell him he was in major trouble for withholding information, but she didn't. She sat there with the note in hand, flipping through papers in her stack. Her eyes glistened at the note, eyeing the lead with some sense of recognition.

"Detective Nazari? Is everything okay?"

"Rohit... this is huge. Thank you for turning it in. This helps so much." She began, digging through the stacks of paperwork. "I know I've seen this handwriting somewhere else." She muttered to herself, dishing the papers out in front of her.

"Here, let me help you." Rohit offered, sitting down next to her, going through the papers. He was too late to help Wren, but at least he owed it to Stella to do the right thing. "Detective, these are all teachers." Rohit pointed out, confused.

"Yes, Rohit. We are investigating teachers. We think one of them may have been romantically involved with Stella and when things went wrong..."

"He killed her."

"Exactly."

"No, Detective. *He* killed her. This handwriting matches the note." Rohit pointed to one of the forms strewn across the table.

He was right, they were a perfect match. Both looked like they were written in a rush. They were borderline scribbles smudged over with ink. A lefty, no doubt. She picked up the page with shaking hands, overwhelmed with excitement over finding the man.

The sound of Donovan's shoes clicked back toward them. She carried two cups of coffee, happy with the caffeine in her body. She went to extend the cup to Detective Nazari when she saw the mess on the table. "What's going on here?"

"We need to see the Econ teacher, Mr. Alcott. He's the guy," Layla announced, more sure of herself than any gut feeling could give her.

Donovan dropped the cups and Layla jumped from the table, abandoning everything to sprint to Mr. Alcott's room at the opposite end of the school. His room, like many others, was dark and locked. They kicked the door open only to find it empty, his bag, papers, and all other signs of him gone for the day.

Donovan pulled her walkie talkie up to her mouth. "I need everyone to be on the lookout for Daniel Alcott, six-foot one, Caucasian male, last seen at Richmond High School."

Footsteps sounded from behind them, and they whipped around, ready to make an arrest right there.

"Woah! Take it easy! I just have some tests to grade." A middle-aged woman said, pushing her keys through the door next to Mr. Alcott's door.

"Ma'am, do you know where Mr. Alcott is?" Donovan asked, desperation causing her voice to get louder and more assertive.

"Danny? Hmm, he probably went home. I think he lives at the edge of Woodbridge park. You know, the one with the big man-made lake. Why do you ask?"

With that, her and Detective Nazari were flying through the front doors and jumping into their squad car. Lights and siren blaring, they were off, leaving Rohit alone again.

With a deep breath, he walked through the empty halls and scrolled through his phone to try to call Wren. She had no reason to answer him, and he didn't expect her to ever want to talk to him again. On the last ring, he heard her breathing and felt his heart instantly melt. "Wren. It's Mr. Alcott. He killed Stella. He's not at the school anymore, so just be on the lookout. Okay?"

"God, I can't believe it. Our Econ teacher? He's a fucking pedophile!" Wren realized, in disbelief. "Thanks for the heads up, Ro."

Just hearing her call him Ro sent butterflies through his body. Oh how he missed her. "I know. He's messed up."

"Wait, Ro." Wren's breathing quickened. "I'm gonna Facetime you." All of a sudden, Wren's face appeared on Rohit's phone screen. Her face was strained, like she was squinting out the window.

He heard the click of the front door being unlocked. He watched her step outside into the sun. "Wren, are you alone right now?" He asked, curious as to why she was acting so off.

"No, everyone else is inside," she replied, her eyes focusing on something. "This car was following me and Asa a little while ago," Wren explained, flipping her

There are two sides to everyone...

camera view to the front, showing a beat-up black pickup truck parked outside of her house.

He watched her get closer to it, checking to see if anyone was inside. Something flashed by in the reflection of the truck's mirror and before he could yell at Wren to run, Mr. Alcott's face came into frame, taking her head in his hand and smashing it against the side of the truck. Rohit screamed and sprinted to his car, turning the keys in the ignition and speeding out of the parking lot, nothing but pure terror taking control of his actions. Wren's phone fell to the ground as Rohit heard the car door open, and Mr. Alcott scooped Wren up and stuffed her into the passenger seat.

Rohit called Asa in a panic, who told everyone else in their friend group, all of whom jumped into their cars and sped through the streets looking for Wren. He called the precinct, reporting Mr. Alcott's whereabouts. He tried choking down his tears because they were blurring his vision. He drove dangerously, willing to risk his own life to save his best friend, the one who deserved the whole world.

Everything he felt for Wren over the years had been elevated. Every kiss on the cheek, every shoulder shove, every random burst of laughter. He felt love and fear and worry and loneliness and love and love and love. He wanted her to be there sitting next to him in his car singing horribly off key to whatever was on the radio. He wanted them to have their families get together for dinner again. He wanted to talk to her about their favorite memories again. He wanted her to be there when he got home from piano lessons, seeing her give Ria some teenage advice. He wanted her to be okay. He wanted her.

He just hoped he could get to her first. And that she wouldn't suffer the same fate as Stella.

And if she did...

He would never, *ever* forgive himself.

She was everything he wanted.

Chapter 27

———

Wren woke up to a pounding headache. The second she opened her eyes she turned and vomited. Her skull felt like she had been hit by a bus, debilitating all movement. When her stomach settled, she turned her head to see where she was and how she had gotten there.

Her eyes were adjusting, trying to focus on her exact location, when she was able to make out Mr. Alcott sitting across from her, fishing through a duffle bag. Wren looked at the ground around her. A tree trunk supported her back and her body laid limp in the dirt. Trees scattered around her, closing in like dark shadows. She pulled herself up, ready to scream for help, hoping to find some energy to run when the unexpected happened. Mr. Alcott began to cry.

"You know I loved her." He whimpered. "Stella. She was something else."

Wren couldn't believe how a man she had been learning from for an entire year had a completely different side to him. She couldn't believe he was anything but a boring divorcée who lived alone and hated his job. But there he was, a grown man, breaking down in front of a student. A student he attacked. Well, the second student he attacked.

"Say something," he commanded, looking over at Wren with pained dark eyes. She could smell the faint stench of liquor coming from his side, slowly unraveling him before her.

"What happened?" Wren found herself asking. She was waiting for the trees to stop spinning around her and to catch her breath.

"She pursued me. She needed some extra help in economics, so I offered to tutor her..." he recalled, holding back tears. "Stella kissed me that day. I knew it was wrong. She was my student... but I was so excited that someone like her was interested in me. I didn't think that would ever happen again." He took a moment to collect himself.

"So, where'd it go wrong?" Wren mumbled, feeling the bump on her skull.

Mr. Alcott looked right up at Wren like she was the reason. His eyes were unforgiving, clear he was drowning in loneliness. "Things were going well for a while, until she started asking me to lower your test scores. I couldn't do it, because you were doing so well. She got angry with me."

"Oh." Wren breathed. "So she was seeing you just to sabotage me?"

Something changed in him. He blinked back the emotions from before, rising, charging at her with a force greater than anger. Wren screamed, and he threw his

There are two sides to everyone...

hand over her mouth, muffling any noise. "Scream like that again and I'll kill you slower. I'll make it hurt."

She winced at the force of his grasp and how his hand threw her head back against the tree, making the forest spin around even faster. He lowered his hand, the bump in her head burning and stinging even more. "I promise I won't scream again," she pleaded, hoping to find some way to make it out of this alive.

"It wasn't all about you. I found her trying to hack into my gradebook and boost her scores. She knew I had some buddies on the board at Columbia, so she repeatedly asked me to put in a good word for her. But it wasn't enough."

"It's hard to change an Ivy League's mind. Stella was desperate to get into any of them. I'm sorry she used you," Wren apologized, hoping that her empathy might buy back her life.

"It wasn't all that. We had some really great moments together. We just had to keep it quiet because no one could find out." He looked back at Wren, like he was toying with some idea in his head, still weighing out the options. "But now you know. That's why I have to kill you." And with that, he pulled a large knife from his duffle bag.

Wren saw how the steel blade glistened, her body flooding with the all too consuming feeling of fear. She saw the change in his eyes slowly becoming more certain of this fate. She would do anything to change it back to her dull econ teacher.

"The police know that you were involved. They found some blood at the crime scene and it didn't match me or

Stella, so it must be yours. The second you're in custody, they're going to test it. Then they'll know everything that happened," Wren explained, regaining some of her strength again.

Just as she thought she might be able to push herself up off of the ground, he lunged at her, pulling her head back by her hair and holding the knife close to her neck. "That's why you should have gone down for this, not me. That's why I called in the anonymous tip that night I saw you and your friends running around. I knew it would be easy to pin it on one of you, but then I saw you and it was *too* easy. You two already hated each other and everyone knew it. I just had to help the police see that. And if you would have been arrested like I had planned, we wouldn't be in this mess!" He growled, pressing the knife's edge into her neck.

His breath was hot and foul in her ear. She squirmed under his greasy skin, but he dug the blade in deeper, making her neck fiery and sear with pain. She cried out as the tip slowly cut below her jaw. Tiny crimson drops dripped onto her neck, slowly forming into little streams. The pain was unbearably long, unlike any sort of release she could feel. It was satanic. She hated him. She wanted it to be over already, but she couldn't give up that fast. She was Wren Clements. She was destined for amazing things, for living life for real, for looking beyond the text-books. She had felt a life that was worth living for, and she was not going to let some sleazy, heartbrokenly disgusting man ruin it for her. She wasn't going to let anyone ruin her. She would make it out of this, bloody and beaten if she had to, but alive.

Alive. She *had* to live.

She felt her fingers feel around the ground for something, anything, to help her get out of his hold. Deep between patches of grass and mud, Wren's fingers closed in around a jagged rock the size of a softball. The pain was making her drowsy and delirious, but she gripped it hard. *Please let this work*, Wren pleaded in her mind. With whatever strength was left in her, she brought it down with a force greater than resentment on Mr. Alcott's head. The knife released from his grasp as he stumbled back to the ground, caught off guard. A small stream of blood dripped down the side of his head.

This is it, Wren thought before pulling herself up and sprinting away.

"HELP!" she screamed as she stumbled through the woods. She had always wondered what it would be like to have no more air in her lungs, but this was not one of those moments. "HELP!" She ran toward any sign of light. She turned her head for a quick second and caught a glimpse of Mr. Alcott trailing after her, knife still in hand. "HELP ME!"

He was a couple yards behind her, but her head started blurring images together. Her legs were on fire and her back was drenched in icy cold sweat. Every nerve was set ablaze, pushing her forward by some force she didn't realize she had left. Dark splotches filled her vision, noises blending together in one hazy breeze. Her very being felt like some sort of hallucination, like her body was shutting down and giving up... surrendering. Then, all of a sudden, she saw images running past her. She heard yelling and glanced back to find Mr. Alcott pinned down on the ground, something silver around his wrists. When she whipped her head forward again, her legs gave out, the black spots meshing into one. The last thing she remembered was a figure running up to catch her before she fell into the person's arms.

"Wren, thank god! You're okay. You're okay, Wren," she heard someone's voice say before giving into the darkness, feeling nothing at all.

There are two sides to everyone...

Chapter 28

The bright fluorescent lights pained her before she even opened her eyes. Her body ached at merely wanting to wake, showing signs of life. Her fingers twitched as she felt something hard clamped around her finger, coming more in touch with reality. A monotone beep sounded every few seconds, the rustling of paper not too far.

Wren opened her eyes, gasping for air, the beeping echoing rapidly as she adjusted to the scene.

"Wren, honey?" Her father squeezed her hand.

"Thank god. I'll get the doctor." Her mother rushed out of the room.

"Dad, everything hurts." Wren choked, her voice adjusting to the movement. Her fingers grazed her throat, feeling a bandage over what used to be a slit on her neck. She retracted them, instantly alarmed, gluing her arm back to her side.

"I know, honey. But you're okay. You're safe now," her father cooed, stroking his thumb along her hand.

"Wren Clements, it's nice to meet you." A doctor stepped into the room following Wren's mother. "You've been through a lot. Do you remember what happened?"

"I remember it all," Wren whispered, memories of the woods, the knife, him... all resurfacing.

"Good. That's really good, Wren." The doctor wrote notes down on her clipboard. "I'm just going to do some extra checks of your vitals and physical responses if that's okay with you."

Wren nodded her head, flinching in pain. Her hand felt the side of her head, fingers brushing along another bandage only to pull them back at the touch as if it had the chance to hurt her again.

The doctor evaluated Wren's bandages, her eyes, and just about everything else. "You have a concussion. Should be gone in ten to fourteen days, but I would take it easy for a few months. You've been hit really hard in the head, so you might experience trouble focusing, some nausea, and you might even get a little forgetful. We gave you some stitches for the cut and fixed your head up. We want to keep you here for the next two days just to keep an eye out for anything else. But you're going to be okay." She smiled.

"That's great, Wren." Her mother sighed, a palm to her chest.

"What happened to Mr. Alcott?" Wren questioned once the doctor left the room.

"He's been arrested and will pay for what he did to you and Stella," her father explained, still holding his daughter's hand. His eyes traveled over her arms and face, his eyes brimming with tears as he glanced at each bruise.

Wren's mother circled around to her other side. "Wren, I am so sorry that this happened. I wish I was there to protect you. I wish that last night didn't happen and you would be okay," her mother remorsed.

"I don't." Wren tried to crack a smile, although it hurt her head. "He got caught. It wouldn't be fair to Stella if he was walking free. And who knows how many more people he was going to hurt. This sucks, but that would have sucked more."

Her parents wrapped their arms around her, making her feel as though her broken pieces were somehow meshed back together. "We love you, Wren," her mother whispered into her hair. In that moment, Wren actually believed her.

That night had been particularly difficult to sleep. Wren had tossed and turned in the hospital bed about a hundred times over before falling into a half slumber. Her head still faintly pulsed in agony despite the pain medication she was taking. Her eyes fell into the blackness of her mind, hoping to find some sort of refuge in her dreams.

There she was again, fingernails digging into the dirt, head bloody from the blow to the head. When she looked up, there he was, standing before her. Mr. Alcott, rifling through his bag, searching for a knife. Then the blade was to her throat, fingers yanking her hair so far back that her eyes stung with fear. The blood dripped back down her burningly cold skin, tingling hot drops of crimson down her front. Then he charged after her through the woods as she screamed. Screamed for anyone.

Wren screamed herself awake. A nurse rushed in, checking Wren's vitals.

"Sorry. Bad dream," Wren whispered, trying to shake the remnants of those memories from her mind.

"Trouble sleeping?" the nurse asked.

Wren nodded and he checked something off on Wren's charts.

"The doctor said you can take a sedative if need be."

Wren nodded, grateful, as the nurse injected another liquid into her IV drip. A couple minutes later, the sedative had crept through her veins and infiltrated her terrorized mind. She fell back into the darkness.

The next morning, Wren woke up to her parents in a scuffle with some nurses and a group of people at the door.

"Just let us see her! We won't wake her!" she heard Tyler's voice plead.

Wren wanted to laugh, happy that her new friends cared about her this much. A huge grin grew across her face. "She's already awake," she announced, watching every head from the doorway turn her way. "Please, come in," Wren invited.

Her parents looked back at Wren with a look of "are you sure?"

She nodded, and her parents left them all alone, making a trip to the cafeteria. Her friends rushed through the door, arms filled with goodies. Asa flocked to her side, reaching for her hand. She took it, all those feelings of excitement rushing back.

"Hi," she breathed.

"Hi," he breathed back.

"Uhhh... should we leave you two alone?" Mia asked, worried that the pair might start making out at the sight of each other.

"No, don't leave! Thank you guys for coming." Wren beamed. Her veins filled with the most energy she had felt in the last day.

"Of course, babe! We wanted to make sure you were feeling okay. How are you doing?" Valerie organized the gifts everyone brought by the window. Wren's dull hospital room was already brightening with the flowers, teddy bears, cards, and extra goodies.

"Better now that you guys are here." Wren looked at each of them, the unlikely gang of friends. But somehow, it didn't feel enough. "Did anyone else come with you?"

"You mean Rohit?" Derek asked, nervously.

"Someone should tell her," Mia stated, eyeing everyone around her.

"Tell me what?" Wren asked, trying to sit up more in her bed.

"What's the last thing you remember, Wren?" Sammy questioned.

"I don't know... I... I remember running from the woods and then everything went dark. Can somebody tell me what's going on?"

A silence hung in the air, the rest of the friends toying with the idea of telling her or if it would be too much for her at the moment.

"The cops knew to go there because of Rohit. He was on Facetime with you when you got abducted, and he called the cops. They knew to lookout for Mr. Alcott's truck," Asa explained.

"Yeah, and Rohit went driving around town like a mad man. He was there when the cops found you and

Mr. Alcott. He said you collapsed in his arms and that's when they called an ambulance," Mia added, rushing to get to the facts.

The words were slowly coming back to Wren. *"You're okay. You're okay, Wren."* She did remember. She had remembered a sense of familiarity in those words. It was Rohit all along.

"Is he okay?"

"He's fine. Just a bit shaken up after seeing you like that," Valerie recounted.

"So you've seen him. Talked to him?"

"He wanted us to give you this." Derek pulled a large bouquet of flowers from the windowsill and placed it on the table in front of Wren.

Wren's heart broke just a crack as she reached out to touch a petal, letting it fall from the flower and onto the table. She felt around the arrangement, fingertips brushing against cardstock, and she plucked it out.

I'm sorry. —Ro

Tears brimmed in Wren's eyes, but she choked her feelings down the best she could. "He didn't think that he should deliver these himself?" Wren asked, tucking the card back into the arrangement.

"I think he was just nervous. He didn't know if you would be more upset if he came," Tyler explained, shrugging.

Wren nodded her head, the pain slowly coming back. "Thank you guys for coming. I'm really sorry. I think I just need to sleep. My meds are making me lethargic."

"No problem. Get some rest, babe." Valerie nodded, gesturing for everyone to leave the room.

They all filtered out, but Asa stayed glued to her side. "Do you want me to leave too?" he asked, his chocolate eyes glistening.

"I don't know."

"Are you *really* okay?"

"I don't know."

"Is there anything I can do to help?" Asa rubbed his thumb along Wren's hand.

Wren thought about how easy it would be to push him away and act like she was Perfect Wren again and could handle these things on her own. But she wasn't that same person. She was done feeling like everything weighed on her shoulders. Things would be okay if she could pass some of that weight off to people who cared for her. And Asa was there for her, looking to take some of that burden.

"I've been getting these nightmares about Mr. Alcott. I wake up screaming... Would it be okay if you just stayed here while I slept? Just for a little bit?"

A soft smile grew across Asa's face. He nodded and said, "Scooch over," sliding himself next to her on her hospital bed. He wrapped his arms around her, letting her head fall on his chest, matching his breathing to hers.

She fell into the closest thing to a peaceful sleep as she let herself be intoxicated by his warmth. She would be okay.

She was okay.

It was all over now.

Chapter 29

———

"Are the nightmares still happening?"

Wren's eyes wandered through the office knick-knacks, eyeing the degrees pinned to the wall. The leather was uncomfortable under her shorts. She checked her watch. She was only fifteen minutes into her hour-long appointment. Therapy was something that she was still getting used to in her third week of being a victim.

"Uh-huh." Wren tried not to think about it too much. The doctor had prescribed her something to help with her sleep, but it was obvious that the PTSD was slowly eating away at her.

"Same one?"

"Can we talk about something else?" Wren had resorted to picking at her nails any time the topic of her attack came up.

Dr. Elliot, her therapist wrote down a couple lines in her notes before closing the notebook. "Okay. Let's talk about your plans."

Wren's eyes lifted from her fingernails to meet her therapist's gaze. "I wasn't aware that I had any plans."

"With deferring a semester at UPenn because of the head trauma and your usual busy nature, I think it would be unwise for you to merely lay around and do nothing."

Wren rolled her eyes at Dr. Elliot. She was getting good at mapping when her therapist would put the notebook and all the other textbook-bullshit away to get real with her. "Did my mother put you up to this?"

"No one put me up to this, Wren."

"She's been nonstop hounding me about how I should just be a part time student at UPenn at the least."

"Is that what you want?"

"No." Wren breathed.

"What *do* you want?" Dr. Elliot countered, looking for some scrap of Wren's opinion.

Wren merely shrugged her shoulders and went back to picking at her nails.

Dr. Elliot sighed, taking her glasses off. A pang of guilt hit Wren, making her direct her attention away from her nails for one second. This woman was just trying to do her job. "What do *you* think I should do?" Wren asked, merely humoring her therapist.

"I can't tell you what to do. Only you can decide that."

"Dr. Elliot, I thought we were done with the textbook responses. C'mon, tell me honestly. Off the record," Wren pressed. She actually found herself curious of what her therapist could possibly advise her to do.

Dr. Elliot sighed again and put her glasses back on. *"Off-the-record,* I think that staying at home is going to be tough for you. We talked before about how much pressure you face at home, and honestly, I think a change of scenery could do you some good. But you need a support system. You can't just up and leave on your own. If you have that, I think it will help you. I think there are too many triggers here. Am I right?" she questioned, already knowing the answer.

"I used to cut myself," Wren confessed.

"Why?"

"Like you said... triggers. But they were different. It was always about not being good enough. Since my attack, since Mr. Al—*he...* since he put that knife to my throat," Wren wiped a tear she didn't know had slipped out, "I just didn't want to anymore."

"It scared you." Dr. Elliot understood.

"Yeah. And now, I don't know what to do, because there's always this push and pull of wanting to be perfect and then thinking that I don't need to be perfect. I just don't know what to do anymore. My life plan has gone to shit, and I don't know why I feel this way."

"Defeated?"

"No," Wren admitted. "Relieved."

"I'm confused. Did you not want to go to UPenn?" Dr. Elliot asked, her notebook open again.

"I did at one point. But I think that I've been playing with this idea in my mind for some time that there must be more. More to life than doing the thing that you think is right. And there's some joy to doing what you really want."

There are two sides to everyone...

Dr. Elliot scribbled in her notebook some more. "And what do you want?"

"I think I need to take your advice... I think I need to leave and find something else. Find a version of myself that is one hundred percent me."

"And a good support system! Let's not forget that," her therapist added, nodding her head.

"I already have one." Wren stated, the first smile during a therapy session forming at the corners of her mouth.

***

The gang met at Sundae's an hour after Wren had sent them a group text to hang out. Asa had gotten into the habit of driving Wren everywhere since her concussion, and he was more than happy to do it. He was ready to take some of the weight off of her shoulders.

"Wren, just wait one second," Asa advised, worried about Wren the second her fingers closed around the handle to get out of the car.

"I'm not gonna pass out or anything. I can get the door on my own," Wren countered, but Asa had already made his way to her side, grabbing her hands to get her back up. She didn't like to admit it, but small things like getting up quickly still made her a little dizzy and the headaches had become just about as normal as breathing.

But she was coping.

"Got you a cookies and cream shake," Derek hollered over from their picnic table outside of Sundae's.

Asa and Wren made their way over as Valerie slid over on the bench to make room for the pair. The gang had been meeting at Sundae's twice a week to catch up on things. They were only a week away from graduation, and Wren had felt out of the loop, missing school for two weeks.

"Thanks, Derek." Wren smiled, taking a sip before passing the shake off to Asa.

"So, what's new?" Mia asked.

"Why do I always have to share first?" Wren rolled her eyes playfully. "Someone else go. Tyler, what's happening with that boy you've been talking to?"

"Casey?" Tyler raised his eyebrows, trying to hide the heat rising in his cheeks. "Yeah." He laughed, rubbing the back of his neck. "We're going out again on Friday. I'm excited."

"You should be." Derek grinned. "My buddy's seeing a college man. You're really growing up." He wiped a fake tear sarcastically from his cheek.

"Alright. Settle down." Tyler laughed. "Mia, you're next."

"New pictures!" She pulled a stack of developed photos out. They passed them around, pointing out ones where they modeled, candid photos of the gang eating ice cream, and many other locations around town.

"Mia, these are great!" Sammy gushed, holding a silhouette picture of herself up.

"Keep that one. I want you to have it," Mia offered, eyeing how Sammy didn't hate herself in a picture for once.

"Thank you." She held the picture to her chest and patted it with her palm.

"I'm really proud of you, Sammy." Mia gave her a hug, which triggered a head turn by everyone. Mia was undoubtedly more comfortable with the group, but they had yet to surpass the physical touch barrier.

Sammy embraced it wholeheartedly. She had found a good support system too. "Thank you," she whispered into Mia's shoulder. "Recovery has been a bitch, but it's the right thing to do."

While Wren couldn't focus on her usual interests like reading due to her concussion, she got better at noticing things about people. She noticed the way that Sammy had more energy in her voice and how Mia was smiling more often. Tyler's phone would buzz, and he would look up grinning. Derek would be speckled with more paint than usual—it was clear that he was especially inspired lately. Valerie was changing her style, finding comfort in a summery European inspired vibe, and Asa... he was still sad that their teenage years were fleeting but smiled through the pain, knowing this was how life was supposed to go.

Life is merely meant to persist. This story might be great, but so might the next one. It was the beauty of the unknown.

"Val, how's the roommate search going?" Derek asked, taking a chunk out of his ice cream.

"Still going." She groaned, bitterly taking a bite out of her cone. "I wish I could just live with someone normal like you guys."

"What? A murder suspect and a group of confused teenagers? We sure would make things *interesting*." Asa laughed.

Valerie choked on her ice cream cone out of a spurt of laughter, launching the group into a hysterical fit.

Wren thought about Valerie moving to London, soaking in the rich history, embracing the culture, wandering unfamiliar streets. She was happy for Valerie, but she found that some part of her wanted that too. The old Wren would have thought things through more thoroughly, but for some reason it seemed to make sense.

"Val, can I talk to you real quick?" Wren asked, already pushing up from the table.

Valerie nodded and got up, meeting Wren under the tree next to Sundae's. "What's up? Are you okay?" she questioned, concern brimming in her eyes.

"I'm fine, Val." Wren giggled. "Okay, so I was talking with my therapist today, and she was telling me how this place is really triggering, and with deciding to not go to UPenn, I need a change of scenery and something to do. And I just can't stay home, not with my mother expecting me to be the same robot of a person. And there's all this money that I would be otherwise using on school, and if you're okay with it—"

"Hold on... Wren, are you saying what I think you're saying?" Valerie asked, eyes widening with each word.

"You said you needed a roommate." Wren smiled, shrugging her shoulders, excitement pumping through her veins.

"Oh my god!" Valerie shrieked, giddy with the turn of events. She hugged Wren, squeezing her so tightly that Wren had to take a step back to stop her head from spinning.

There are two sides to everyone...

"I can't guarantee I'm the normal roomie that you're looking for." Wren giggled again. "But my therapist said I need a good support system. And you, Valerie Scott, are just about the best person I know. I can't be here anymore. I want to see what else is out there for me. And I want to do it by your side." Wren looked into Valerie's eyes.

"What about your parents? What are they gonna think?"

"Oh, they're gonna hate this idea," Wren started, "but I've been a good daughter for seventeen years. Life's too short to do something that you don't want to do." She winked. "I'll work it out with them. Don't worry."

Chapter 30

Graduation was in a week.

Wren was still getting daily lectures from her mother about her decision to go abroad. Her mother was worried for her sanity, and her father was worried for her health, but she grew tired of Pennsylvania. It was official. She and Valerie signed a lease for a flat in London and had plane tickets booked in early August.

Wren was putting her shoes on to go out for a walk. She couldn't run or bike again for a while without getting a massive wave of vertigo that scared her parents. Some days she would struggle to get out of bed, but others were better.

Sometimes she would walk down the street and back, letting her body take full control over where it wanted to go, but she found herself walking right to Rohit's door that day. Her finger shook as she took a deep breath before ringing the doorbell.

She was about to turn around and keep walking, but in a minute, Rohit was at the door. Every emotion poured out through his glance. He fumbled with the handle and felt like his heart was beating out of his chest. He didn't deserve to, but he took a step toward her and threw his arms around her, relieved to see his best friend standing there on his front porch.

Like magnets, her arms wrapped around him too, feeling how warm he was against her. She missed that feeling. No, she missed him. "Do you want to walk with me?" Wren asked when he let her go.

He nodded, closing the front door.

They walked down the street and sat by a quiet creek. Wren felt the grass through her fingers, hoping to enjoy the summer budding inside, but instead she retracted her fingers in a panic. That feeling of digging her hands in the dirt was too familiar. She was immediately brought back to the memory of her in the woods, head against a tree, searching for something to defend herself.

"Are you okay?" Rohit asked, catching her moment's panic.

Wren tried to gain control over her breathing. "Just going through it a bit. I'll be okay."

"Wren?"

She knew him so well still that she could already tell what he was going to say, just by the look on his face.

"I'm sorry."

"I know, Ro."

"No, I don't think you understand. You would have never been in that situation if I hadn't been so scared. It's my fault." He buried his face in his hands, unable to bring himself to look at her.

She reached over to his hands and pulled them away from his face. "Hey, I get it. It's not okay, and I don't know if I can ever entirely forgive you, but I understand. I just really missed my best friend," Wren admitted. She was beginning to feel more like herself again.

"I missed you too. And I'm sorry if I messed everything up when I told you how I felt."

"That was pretty selfish, Ro."

"I know... I shouldn't have kissed you. I don't know what I was thinking. I'm sorry," he apologized profusely.

"Don't apologize for how you feel. Don't regret telling me. I just need you to know that I do love you." He looked up at her. "But not like that," Wren explained. This was the talk she was dreading.

"I get it. You're with Asa now. He's good for you." Rohit shrugged, hurt, but genuine.

"He is. And I like him a lot."

"Good. You really do deserve the best, Wren." He squeezed her hand.

"You do too. I'm just not her. You're going to meet so many amazing people in college and experience so many crazy things. I'm sorry that our night out wasn't what you were looking for."

"I don't regret that night."

"What?" A wave of confusion washed over Wren. "But that night we fought, you said—"

"I know what I said," Rohit interjected. "But I think I said it to hurt you. I was just bitter, and I saw you and Asa getting close. But the more I accepted that something wasn't going to happen between us, I realized that the night wasn't a total waste. I still had fun. And more than anything, I was happy that you enjoyed yourself."

Wren smiled, remembering the night that somehow felt like a lifetime before.

"Anyway, I'm looking forward to visiting you in Philly for some more wild nights." He hit his shoulder against hers like old times.

Wren sat up straighter, the realization kicking in. "Oh, Ro... I didn't tell you."

"Tell me what?" His eyes were searching hers for what she was so nervous to say. "You're not going. Are you?" He realized.

She shook her head. "At first, I was going to take a semester's leave because of the concussion, but after a while it just seemed like that dream died. I don't want that life anymore. I want to try new things, and I can't do that unless I leave Philly. I decided that I'm going to London with Valerie."

"Woah... You never talked about wanting to go to London." He tried to make sense of the words she was dishing out.

"I know... but it's different. And I need that," Wren reassured herself, trying to choke back the fact that she was going to miss Rohit so much.

He nodded, staring off into the distance. It was silent for some time until he let out a chuckle. "How on earth did you convince your parents to let you go to London?"

A grin stretched across Wren's face, bringing the softest touch of warmth to her cheeks. "A contract." She winked.

And just like that, it was all behind them. The fighting, the secrets, the feelings. They let it all go with a burst of laughter. It was like old times.

Because no matter what, they loved each other.

And when you love someone, you make the things that sometimes hurt... work.

Acknowledgments

Writing a book has been a journey, a dream, and sometimes even a pain in the ass. There were so many times when I thought imposter syndrome would take over and I could just crawl under the safety of my bedsheets and give up. But then something amazing happened... I discovered how supportive my family, friends, and community (not to forget the strangers from TikTok) were and how they believed in me and my dream. They trusted me to tell a story, and it was their endless encouragement that helped me write *Everything You Wanted*. For my whole life, I have just wanted to be a storyteller, and this dream would have stayed tucked away in the pages of my notebook if it weren't for you all.

Thank you first and foremost to my family for encouraging me to write ever since I fell in love with stories as a child. Thank you to my father, who showed me that writing is a beautiful gift that is in our blood. Thank you to my mother, who is my biggest cheerleader and can always calm me down when I'm spiraling. Thank you to my sister, Neha, who promised that she would actually read this one.

Thank you to my third grade teacher, Mrs. Devlin, who told me that I should be an author when I grew up. Mrs. Devlin, I finally did it.

In addition, I am so incredibly grateful to many others who have helped me reach my dreams. Thank you to:

Alisha Sehgal, Grace Lewis, Thomas Luu, Brianna Nguyen, Shivang Patel, Tessa O'Donnell, Adara Morganstein, Manjunath Gurubasavaiah, Latha Channarasappa, Cait Jacobs, Indu Rajesh, Ragu R, Venkataram Krishnier, Naveen Srinivasan, Michelle McLarnon, Katie McCollum, Diane Giglietti, Diane McTamney, Srikar Katta, Ashley Cavuto, Eric Rivera, Jen Du, Melite Scherzinger, Prasad Ramnath, Indu Janardanan, Padmavathi Chivukula, Sruthi Manivannan, Venkat Subramaniam, Priyanka Patel, Neeraja Madulapally, Surekha Jituri, Zev Burton, Giuliana Carrozza, Najuk Patel, Anami Patel, John Dimase, Meena Avin, Vijayakumar V, Goutam Challagallas, Srilatha Panjala, Dhilan Patel, Bridget Gallagher, Santhi Nithi, Caroline Doyle, Meera Boghara, Alexandra Chiu, Sarah Bryant, Gauri Deshmukh, Nirali Doshi, Jessica Cascone, Rachel Wiener, Eric Koester, Alka Rathod, Meg Burke, Raman Sampath, Vimala Sivakumar, Megan Kirk, Renae Leonard, Sujatha Prakash, Anup Chaudhry, Revathi Subramanian, Jackie Galang, Rama Malaviya, Erika Anuzelli, Morgan Anderson, Eric Wolfe, Sadanand Morbad, Sunitha Venkatanarayanan, Jeff Eshleman, Ruth Hay, Christen Nino De Guzman, Aarati Martino, Jenny Sosa, Candace Kilstein, Kelly Sullivan, Tali-Jade Goodwin, Keya Patel, Sara Stavely, Noah Clemens, Christina Thomas, Olivia Liu, Emma Austin, Valerie Lane, Asha Kunchakarra, Amelia Patterson, Rafi Naseer, Puneeth Guruprasad, Nalla Mankuski, Ria Bhandarkar,

Prabal Johri, Hemant Kumar, Deepa Luitel, Linette Ortiz-Barnes, Priya Patel, Stephanie Midolo, Ashwini Kumar, Shannon Severin, Grace Baker, Julia Park, Julie Ritsick, Courtney Sabanas, Melissa Glenn-Fleming, Palak Patel, Isabelle Baldi, Emily Henry, Sharon George, Marcella Smith, Nivita Chaliki, Sarah Tennant, Nikhil Patel, Next Gen Community, Samantha Berdel, Cheyenne Bluett, Haley Newlin, Lindsay Webb, Anna Kmiec, Destiny Davis, Charlie Hilpert, Deanna Llorente, Ruby Cunney, Margaret Ronolder, Abigail Doyle, Makennia Gaalswyk, Jana Geiser, Estephania Campa, Katelynne Wittmier, Kat Latham, Moya Carter, Paula Berweger, Jennifer Rudacille, Denaé Robinson, Trevina Martinez, Neeraj Periwal, Abby Posner, Nicole Casta, Katie Whalin, Cassandra Bergantim, Sierra Morgan, Ali Alcazar, Shelby Westenskow, Jackson Cubba, Crystal Cabello, Jasmine Bradley, Mollie Hiss, Eden McCain, Sukhmani Kaur, Izzy Leasure, Reina McClure, Elena McKenney, Claire Hartmann, Caitlin Cantwell, Gibran Silva, Raya Maitland, Oli Parlato, Sadie Fox, Cheyenne Perkins, Sara Stangl, Natalie Marie Brown, Bianca Wiegerink, Allison Franklin, Ashlyn Macomber, Brianna Duffin, Maria Rabaino, Ashley Hamilton, Skyii Leslie, Liz Smith, Meena Pelgar, Rachel Klingler, Kaitlyn MacMillan, Sara Yoe, Rachel Matlack, Marisa Rotolo, Alyssa Berger, Troy Johnson, Caitlyn Kaye, Warishah Qandil, Jasmine Wu, Madison Fell, Sarai Zarate, Jessica Powers, John Cavuto, Molly Schaff, Jamie Wei, Jax Turner, Kathy Ramirez, Alicia Marcoux, Amelia Neuber, Emilie Christensen, Caroline O'Keefe, Adrianna D Penna, Koda Kiser, Brenda Robinson, Sean Groh, Sarah Keller, Jaci Driscoll, Brynn Spoon, Aicia Alkatheeri, Halee Kewish, Ariana Neceski,

Molly Sabido, Kalilah Stein, Gina Affleck, Morgan Hall, Beth Whitehead, Brooke Bengle, Hailey Wortham, Miko Coakley, Max Egan, Arielle Noel, Shwe Phue, Kansas Jade Nicholson, Stefanie Coughlin, Ipsita Tingi, Jennifer Augastine, and Victoria Barahona.

Thank you for believing in me. It truly means the world to me.

Made in the USA
Columbia, SC
13 May 2021